AF531263

The Garden Path

The Miseducation of a City

Andre M. Perry

UNO PRESS

Printed in the USA
Library of Congress Control Number: 2010942215
ISBN 13: 978-1-60801-048-6

Book design:
Lindsay Maples & Creighton Durrant

Cover photo by the author

UNO PRESS
University of New Orleans Publishing
Managing Editor, Bill Lavender
http://unopress.org

To Mom and Mary: I Love You.

Contents

Foreword

The phrase "being led down the garden path" means to be misdirected, hoodwinked or mislead. The psycholinguistic definition of the garden path is a misinterpretation based upon our preconceived notions.

In my twenty years (and counting) of working in the field, the question, what is higher education, has stayed on my mind like an unrequited dream. I'm not talking about the recognized arrangement of postsecondary institutions, which could use some reimagining. I have been chasing the concept of education as an ideal, a higher order standard.

As a descendent and student of those whose participation in the process of learning was once considered criminal activity, I have always viewed education as a North Star of sorts. Education is the great escape. Its acquisition is so basic, that one cannot literally conceive of living a quality life without it. In this regard, education is a social virtue similar to justice. Education must ground individuals and institutions so that communities can reach their highest potential. I believe that by reaching for higher education we create institutions, curriculums and communities befitting of the ideal. Therefore, scholars and practitioners must explicate a concept of higher education in their writings, policies, and institutions.

One of the most prominent American scholars who provided a clear philosophical vision of what I consider higher education was John Dewey. John Dewey famously said, "education is not preparation for life, education is life itself." If this is true, then community and interpersonal interactions are our primary teachers. Education is not only the math lesson; it's the walk passing the blighted property to the museum. Education is in the enactment of our housing policies. It's in the exchange with our servers at restaurants. Education is the kind hello from the bus driver. Education is exchanged between ex-convicts and their sons. Education is the school board meeting where diatribes are thrown like spears. So when you hear or ponder the question what's wrong with education, don't reflexively look towards public schools; also look at how we live our lives as a community.

The setting of one of my most enduring lessons took place on a blue-carpeted staircase in my childhood home. Mom and I gawked at its peak, which was braced by white balusters and a weathered oak handrail. Hand in hand, we counted each step and made our ascent to the top. Mom methodically and patiently counted, "One, two, say two, two, three, four." Despite our raucous laughter and my inexact counting, we were captivated by a perfect blend of movement, progression, learning, love, and most importantly struggle. I hadn't completely mastered walking stairs at that point. My legs could barely hurdle their height. Completely drunk with inexperience and lost without a guiding hand, I found balance through learning with my best friend.

Eventually, I grew bold enough to contribute to the discussion, "Five, six, six, six." Mom politely got me back on course and reset my position on the stairs. Even with my limited know-how, making it to the top never seemed difficult. No error became a mistake; no slip became a fall; and disciplined thinking wasn't so strict. She was there for me. All we wanted was to calculate the stairs together.

I don't quite remember when I mastered my first math lesson, when I could climb stairs with ease, when the mountain became a staircase, or saying goodbye before my mother passed away, but I will always remember our rise together.

The Garden Path is about views of education reform from inside and outside the schoolhouse, which is the book's epicenter. The book narrates education within the lives of schooling's primary stakeholders: students, families, teachers and administrators. It also critically examines this latest wave of reform using the New Orleans post-Katrina context as a stage to examine different experiences and positions in the contentious battles around education.

This fictional narrative is primarily a story of two high school students' (Loren and Katura) journey to college and an administrator's (Dr. Isaac Boyd) efforts to get them there. The Miseducation of a City is the first of three parts in The Garden Path series beginning with the students' ninth and tenth grade years, culminating in the students' first-year in college. The first book draws heavily from the first three years of the post-Katrina reform explosion, which exaggerates other cities' efforts to make radical shifts in educational systems and outcomes.

The Garden Path's stories and characters are predicated on my experiences in schools, particularly during my time as Associate Dean of the University of New Orleans' College of Education and Human Development and CEO of the Capital-One UNO Charter Network. I also draw upon my own experiences as a student. Many of the characters may seem familiar to those ensconced in the New Orleans context. Certainly, some of the scenes are historical. However, there are no direct biographies in the text. I created composite characters based on people from across the country. The chronology also does not flow with the factual timeline of events. I intentionally created a piece of fiction to place more emphases on the question of where do we go from here as opposed to who did what to who?

What I loved about writing in fictional form was the freedom it allowed me to weave multiple arguments and perspectives into a dynamic, existential narrative. The shrill of reformer's rampant boosterism and educational preservationist's abject resistance towards change make it difficult to hear practical and ethically sound solutions. I believe the inability to find compassionate solutions is a primary symptom of being miseducated. Being able to hear ourselves collectively and totally is essential if the ultimate goal is to create educated communities. I hope the text raises the multiple voices that I hope one day will form a transformative chorus.

I would like to thank my wonderful family for living in my imagination. My wife Joia, and children Jade, Carlos and Robeson are the fuel to my fire. I would like to thank everyone in the entire University of New Orleans/Capital One-UNO Charter Network family. I work with one of the most caring and intelligent faculty in the country. In particular, I would like to thank James Meza for planting seeds of opportunity all across the New Orleans metropolitan area. Thank you Dr. Vera Triplett and Mr. Stephen Osborn for your remarkable hard work and dedication to children. Without the steady hand of my graduate students, this project could not have been completed. Thank you Rashida Govan, Kelly Owens, Victoria Palmisano, Ann Plicque and Franz Reneau. You are the next generation of faculty members. You make us proud. In particular, Ann Plicque helped edit the manuscript from start to finish. Her beautiful mind enhanced the book tremendously.

The Garden Path

The Miseducation of a City

Rainclouds, Adam's Apples and Honorariums

I landed in New Orleans on a Tuesday evening in May of 2004. It was the third stop of my three-week get-a-job tour. Upon learning of my visit, a close friend who worked at a local technical college invited me to speak at his institution's graduation. Between the prospect of a job and a much-needed honorarium, a great deal of hope rode along with me on this trip.

From Washington to New Orleans, I struggled to recall the face of Dr. Warren Morris, dean of the college of education and chair of the search committee. He told me we had met at a professional meeting a few years earlier. Professors require recognition and I didn't want my memory to jeopardize my chances. After I examined the college's website, I still couldn't remember his face. I worried the entire two-and-a-half hour flight. I hoped urgency would jog my memory as the plane's tires screeched to a landing. Upon deplaning, I searched intently for his face. Fortunately, Dr. Morris' waving saved me. The fifty-something-year-old white male stood erect like a military man. Still, he possessed an ease that most white males didn't carry around black men, particularly around those they just met. I could tell immediately that our conversation would move rapidly.

After university job interviews where livestock outnumbered

people with dreadlocks, seeing people of color made me optimistic. As we strolled towards baggage claim, it was obvious that black people lived here. All the storefront employees were black; the cleaning crew. Some Transportation Security Administration supervisors were white, but black hands clutched every broom. That part of the arrangement felt sadly familiar.

"Hey bay-bay."

Background voices colored my black-and-white view. The folksy dialect attracted me. Warmth wove through the melodic drawl.

"How ya doin bay-bay," asked the dark janitorial worker with scarred shins.

Her voice and her legs seemed to move in unison. I looked at her face, her eyes. The blue rings around her irises, along with her legs, reminded me of my mother.

I said, "I'm well. How are you," and she smiled a smile of universal welcome.

After Dr. Morris hastened my pace with a few pleasantries to remind me of our appointments, he pointed out vivid murals of jazz icons who had played the town. The aging airport showed off bits of city history, and mom-and-pop kiosks flanked the aisle toward baggage claim. I imagined how many music greats commemorated in paint, film and stone might've walked the same floor.

In the parking lot humidity harshly swaddled me. It was if I'd swallowed a hot raincloud. Dr. Morris laughed at my expression.

"Whew. It's a tad bit warm," I said, grinning weakly.

He chuckled as we walked to his car. I felt like I was swimming.

Driving away from the terminal, I marveled at the palm trees and French Quarter men's club advertisements from huge billboards. I noticed the vibe of the vehicles, their license plates, and wondered what their drivers listened to. Dr. Morris tried to play tour guide and talk over the cool air rattling from the dashboard. I wanted to slow his words by opening the window. I reminded myself this was his car, and he chaired the search committee.

"Do you want to go to the hotel or see the area around the university?"

I gushed, "Do you mind? I don't want to impose. You probably have more important things to do than drag me around."

"I don't mind. Everything is close." Dr. Morris looked in his rearview mirrors and veered left. Friends familiar with New Orleans told me I would notice the Spanish and French architecture when I entered the city. I didn't know if Dr. Morris meant to take the St. Bernard Avenue exit, but it didn't represent the European architecture I'd expected.

As we exited the ramp, I interrupted Morris's air-conditioner-muffled statements about my interview schedule and asked, "What is that?"

Dr. Morris said, "That's the St. Bernard."

It was the largest housing development I could remember seeing.

I shouldn't have been surprised. The usual neighbors to an urban university were projects and other impoverished areas. The St. Bernard, only two miles away from the university, provided a different backdrop. Distressed yellow bricks seemed to stretch for miles. Nothing but dark faces were in this population. No white supervisors, no Creoles— only deep brown people. They expressed the range of humans stuck here. I saw smiles, pain, dazed looks, hip-hop youth and drunks. The denizens gazed inside our car with the same astonished looks I gave them.

People are much more significant than architecture, and

the view would have been more depressing if I had paid closer attention, but plastic grocery bags and fast-food containers that rolled across the recently cut grass like tumbleweeds distracted me.

Where were the carefree faces, fun-filled groups, parades, and jazz funerals I had read about? Where were the merriment, debauchery and impromptu street bands that were supposed to welcome me to the Big Easy? I wanted to see people and that's what I got. I saw the boys who looked like me fifteen years ago, and they appeared to be in uniform. All wore white T-shirts, dreadlocks and sagging, oversized Dickies. They should have been in somebody's classroom— high school or college— but it appeared they kept a peculiar watch along these walkways.

Our slow-motion drive piqued my peripheral vision. Across the street beyond the St. Bernard gates stood another throng. These folks worked a corner snowball shop. Cars surrounded the anchored ice cream truck. A steady stream of locals avoided traffic to get their treat. Dr. Morris nearly hit someone as he headed to the shop. The white cups and rainbow-colored ice drew my attention. The hues of people complemented the colors of snowball-filled spoons. The snowballs were obviously popular enough to attract everyone to the stand, including Dr. Morris.

"You've never had a New Orleans snowball. You want one?"

Sensing that 'no' would be inappropriate, I said, "Allow me to treat us both."

We waited in line about ten minutes, and eventually ate leaning against his car door. The projects provided an obvious discussion piece.

The dean said, "We need to move students from here to the university— so close but so far away."

"Seems like a heavy lift. Maybe it would be easier to move the university to the projects."

"The university is probably heavier."

He looked in the university's direction and swallowed a spoonful of Blueberry Surprise.

Dean Morris continued, "We're scheduled to open the first charter school in Louisiana, if that's what you're talking about."

"Interesting. When is it going to open?"

"In a few months— August. The planning has begun. How do you feel about charter schools?"

Knowing the opening required the dean's full endorsement, I replied, "They provide an opportunity to help improve education for struggling schools."

He laughed. "Good answer."

Before we finished our snowballs, we drove through adjacent neighborhoods. He drove a few blocks and made a left onto Bancroft Drive. The scene changed from housing projects to chateaus alongside a peaceful bayou.

"This is where I live."

"Wow, these homes are beautiful."

"I grew up less than a mile from here. I went to a Catholic school down the street. My mother was a secretary at the University. On Sundays, my family would drive up and down this street looking at these homes."

We stopped in front of his house, which was previously owned by a wealthy businessman. It was a California Bungalow style, sprawling two-story home fit more for a college president. The U-shaped design allowed residents and guests to view sunsets on the bayou. Beautiful stone steps led to doors that seemed as wide as the street. It had to be nearly 10,000 square feet.

"If this is how professors live in New Orleans, I'm in," I said.

After making a few stops in nearby predominantly white,

middle-class neighborhood of Lakeview and the black, middle-class Pontchartrain Park, we breezed through the university and headed to the hotel.

The university housed me a stone's throw from the French Quarter, on Carondelet and Canal, a block off Bourbon. Dr. Morris drove through the Central Business District and up and down some Quarter streets. Compared with my most recent recruitment trip in Iowa, strip bars and antique shops were the "corn" in this town. I tried to pay attention to Dr. Morris's closing statements about my interview day, but second-hand lamps, paisley throws, and restaurants were more exciting. As we exited the Quarter for the hotel, I looked in the rearview mirror as if I were leaving an old lover. Dr. Morris followed and made sure I checked in safely. I assured him I would be fine, and bid him adieu.

The bags barely hit my hotel room floor before I rushed back outside to Bourbon Street. As I approached, the sights and sounds entranced me. A brass band's raw music charmed me toward the corner of Canal and Bourbon. As I moved closer, the odor of vomit, urine and beer blunted my enthusiasm. Still, the local talent washed away some of the street stench.

The show began on Bourbon. I walked through a thick crowd gathered around a brass band. A spirited version of "I'll Fly Away" was in progress.

"I'll fly away, oh Lordy, I'll fly away."

I loved the song. I found myself catching the offbeat second-line dance the music spurred. There was a rhythm to New Orleans. I had to catch it and dance.

"Where are you playing," a fifty-something tourist with a black short-sleeved shirt, faded black cargo pants and green Crocks, asked passionately as I moved through the crowd.

It took me a moment before I realized the question was directed at me. Dance sweat dripped from his wire-rimmed glasses.

I replied, "I'm not an entertainer."

He nodded, closed his eyes and awkwardly moved to the bass drum.

After spending enough time walking the streets and getting used to the sights, I stopped at the House of Blues, but no acts were scheduled. Since the house was dark, I decided to eat. My Creole server displayed her breasts as if they were on the menu. After perusing the offerings, I noticed she also displayed an Adam's apple. I said to myself, This is not what I wanted to see. I ordered a grilled chicken sandwich, fries and a Diet Coke, ate my meal, and walked back to my hotel.

* * *

Dr. Morris picked me up the next morning. We drove through a sleepy French Quarter to grab a cup of coffee, and I felt lucky to have had a good night's rest. In between the chit-chat, I kept reflecting on how important it was to land this job. I'd broken up with my fiancée a few weeks before graduation. My bills were as high as my anxiety. My other interviews yielded no offer yet. More importantly, this was the only gig in a chocolate city.

At the college of education two women students comprised a welcome committee. They offered refreshments and gave me a brief tour of campus.

"Where are you from?"

"Why New Orleans?"

I fielded and answered questions most of the walk. Buildings were mentioned almost as afterthoughts. The campus looked liked it had missed a few state appropriations. Its structures seemed stuck in the 1970s. Similar to my House of Blues waitress, the university was a WWII Navy base in drag. Converted in 1958, the campus still conveyed an austere hardness that was only offset by a colorful array of students. Asians, blacks, whites, Indians and other cultural groups gave the campus a scholastic sense and feel. I didn't mind the minimalist décor because it lacked the bearded statues of old-school "distinction" and "charm" I'd seen elsewhere. Living people trumped hallowed ivy walls and made this place new-school beautiful.

My tour circled back to the college of education. The search committee would meet with me before I met the rest of the faculty. The committee seemed excited about my candidacy. Effusive smiles, head nods, and thank yous were dizzying. Their cordiality seemed excessive. Anxiety gave way to a false sense of security.

After the search committee meeting, I presented my research as well as I could. The faculty seemed responsive. After answering every question I could, I mentally pumped my fist in exhilaration.

After a morning with faculty, students and administrators, four faculty committee members and the dean decided to take me off-campus to lunch in the Quarter. They chose a swanky, up-market restaurant where portions were generous. I ordered a steak and got one with crawfish on top. I ordered iced tea, but red wine appeared. I remembered reading you should never drink at an interview. I declined the insistent urging that it was OK to have a glass. I felt foolish after witnessing the committee members share several bottles and whisk away the glass I'd refused.

After lunch, I asked to visit other educational institutions in the area before going to my speech at the community college that evening. Dr. Morris respectively escorted me to Tulane University and Delgado Community College, as well as Joseph Rainey High School. He believed I would want to visit these schools to feel the lay of the land.

The visits to Tulane and Delgado met my expectations. I was familiar with the institutions from professional newspapers, conferences and colleagues. I really wanted to see a high school to get a flavor for local teachers and students. After visits to the postsecondary institutions, Dr. Morris drove me to Rainey, which was one of the lowest performing schools in the state.

As we drove down Esplanade Avenue, I gawked at the French and Spanish architecture. I estimated the homes were at least as old as the magnificent oaks, whose muscular roots buckled sidewalks to make room. The oaks were adorned with moss and "earrings" of Mardi Gras beads. The magnificent trees seemed to grow into the homes' white columns. Their limbs could be viewed from living room porches. As I gawked, I thought these were the types of homes that came from cheap labor and very little tax collection.

From afar, Joseph Rainey High School looked like a huge, more distinguished home on the block. As soon as I thought we were headed to a school of equal value, red and blue police lights interrupted my reverie. The building's architecture reeked of the old money that built it; the inside reeked of longtime poverty and neglect.

We walked up the stairs of the front entrance between four armed guards who talked leisurely to themselves and to students. No one stopped us. We walked in the front door, which was not the main entrance, but it did have a desk and sign-in sheet. The dates on the log were from a month earlier, so I assumed the entrance was used for special events. As Dean Morris escorted me to the principal's office I saw students walking and talking in the halls as if between classes.

The school's main office felt like a Greyhound bus station. A hodgepodge of people waited to talk with Principal Ronald Mabrie.

The front office worker sounded and looked irritated that we joined the group.

"Can I help you?"

Dr. Morris said, "I'm here to see Mr. Mabrie." The front office person turned to her right, sighed and yelled, "Mr. Mabrie!"

She finally asked us, "What's your names?"

"Dr. Morris and Dr. Boyd from the University of New Orleans."

She yelled again, "Dr. Morris would like to see you."

She opened a three-ring binder and said, "Please sign in."

As we signed the visitor's log, Dr. Morris extended his hand and reintroduced himself. She sluggishly said, "Ms. Robinson."

Mr. Mabrie walked out smiling and said, "Dr. Morris! To what do I owe the pleasure of your visit?"

"I want to introduce you to Dr. Isaac Boyd."

Mr. Mabrie appeared to be a disheveled gentleman. This Creole, fifty-something principal was like an old woman adjusting her wig, as Mabrie attempted to straighten his oversized trousers and stick out his chest. His loose, twisted tie revealed a designer label, but his rolled up sleeves showed deep yellow stains near the cuffs. His red eyes suggested his day was long and tiring.

As if to uselessly chastise his assistant's behavior, Mabrie said, "Thank you, Ms. Robinson."

He told two of the parents waiting for him, "As soon as I speak with Dr. Morris and Dr. Boyd, I will see you."

He then told Ms. Robinson, "Please call Juron and Kaylen to

wait with their mothers."

One of them said, "Have you found Juron's paperwork from his last school?"

Mr. Mabrie said, "Give me ten minutes, Ms. Richard," pronouncing it in the French manner 'Ree-chard.' The other mother said, "I've got to go to work in ten minutes. I've been waiting thirty. I've already called in, but this isn't helping me keep my job."

Mr. Mabrie, gently replied, "I'll be right with you and if need be speak to your supervisor."

He then asked the dean, "How may I help you?"

"Dr. Boyd is interviewing with the university and would like to meet some of your students."

Mabrie turned to me. "Where's home?"

"University of Maryland, College Park, but I'm from Pittsburgh."

"The Steelers, huh."

I smiled and said, "That's right."

Mr. Mabrie laughed and said, "We'll give you a few years, then you'll get with the real black and gold," referring to the New Orleans Saints' football team's colors.

"What makes you think I'm not with the real black and gold now?"

"This is a Catholic town. We'll convert you." Mabrie was cordial. He quickly asked me to talk with his students. As he examined my long dreadlocks, he said, "It will be good for our students to see a young, black, accomplished male. Talk to the civics class in Room 104." We opened the door wide enough for Dean Morris and me to peek inside.

The security guard we passed, asked, "You goin' to talk to the kids?"

I said, "A few words."

She added, annoyed, "They need someone to talk to them."

I turned my attention to the classroom. The door slowly swung open. We stood at the class's periphery. Mabrie moved close to the teacher and spoke as Dean Morris and I stood at the door.

The majority of approximately thirty students barely noticed us when we walked inside. Two groups hovered around two computers at the rear of the room.

Before I knew it, Mabrie walked toward me and said, "Ms. Hogan will take it from here. Nice to have met you. I'm sure I'll see more of you." He then left.

Ms. Hogan seemed excited, rose from her desk, straightened her clothes and attempted to capture the students' attention.

"Class, we have visitors."

Much of the class turned their heads to look Dr. Morris and me over. The clash of the dreads and the bowtie drew some interest. Ms. Hogan raised her voice and tone to slightly below yelling to direct the children off the computers.

One student said, "Give me a second."

Ms. Hogan sharply replied, "Move away from the computer and listen."

The student rose but continued to type. Ms. Hogan moved as if she were going to storm to the computer, but the child said, "OK, OK," as he walked, hunched over, to a nearby empty desk. He slouched and looked at his shoes. By the bored expressions, I knew I would lose the audience I had captured with my dreadlocks and neckwear. Ms. Hogan also recognized the shrinking window of opportunity and quickly introduced me.

"This is Dr. Boyd from the University of Maryland. He is going to talk to you about success through education."

She sat down. The introduction was wide open. I expected

Ms. Hogan to give an artful opening about being a young black scholar or about overcoming odds. She probably followed orders and relayed the message given to her. I reminded myself I had interrupted her class.

Taking my cue I gave out a big, "Good afternoon." The students returned a lukewarm response. I sensed that repeating "good afternoon" until the class reciprocated my enthusiasm would not play well, so I introduced myself.

"My name is Dr. Isaac Boyd," I said. As I regurgitated the bio I'd sent with my vitae to prospective colleges and universities, a diminutive girl giggled. I smiled back as I tried to acknowledge what I thought to be a sign of immature admiration. However, as I continued to list my background, her giggle elevated to a chuckle at the mention of my graduate education. Before I could get to my work background, a hearty laugh was followed by a bold pronouncement. The girl belted out, "You ain't no doctor!"

The class erupted in laughter. Confused and somewhat saddened, I looked to Dean Morris for a hand. He smiled and tilted his head as if to say, "This is what you're dealing with." I looked at the teacher, but she joined the students laughing. This went on for almost two minutes. Two minutes is a long time to be ridiculed. The first ten seconds was cute. The last ten bruised my ego. Nevertheless, I waited for the mirth to wane.

I folded my arms like a salty preacher, looked sternly at the girl who attempted to tell me what I wasn't and said, "If you can't see me as a doctor, you certainly can't see yourself as one." The reply silenced any residual giggles.

"What is your name young lady?"

Unafraid, the girl quickly answered, "Jarnee."

"What is your last name Jarnee?"

"Prevost."

"Where are you from, Dr. Prevost."

"Uptown."

"Dr. Prevost, do you know what a doctor of philosophy is?"

"Someone who takes care of people." I looked at her for a couple of moments and extended the question to the rest of the class. "Do any of you know what a doctor of philosophy is?"

One student said, "A nurse."

I responded, "No, you're thinking of a physician. Physicians have M.D.s, medical degrees. I am a doctor of philosophy. If anyone asks, Ph.D.s are the *real* doctors." Knowing I planted a seed, I continued. "Ph.D.s graduate from doctoral, academic studies in a particular field. Does anyone know how you earn a doctorate?"

The curiosity and ignorance silenced the room. I explained why I chose to pursue a doctorate and how. Then I remembered I had my regalia in the car for my upcoming speech. I quickly turned to Dr. Morris to discretely ask for his keys and take over while I got my gown and hood. I excused myself from the class.

"I have something to show you." I sprinted down the front stairs of the school and noticed the parents still arguing with Principal Mabrie. I saw one student in a police car and others hanging out on the corners watching the drama instead of engaging with class. When I reached Dr. Morris's car I asked a student not to lean on it. I opened the door and grabbed the black garment bag.

I ran past the security checks, guards and parents and back to the classroom. I carefully took out my bright, red robe from my alma mater. I held it in front of me and gathered its hood.

A student blurted out, "It looks like my preacher's robe."

I said, "Good observation. Now why do you think that is?" Students waited for my answer. I gave a brief history of higher education. I explained how many of American higher education traditions started in the old, cold monasteries of Europe. "Preachers and professors both pursue truth and needed to stay warm doing it."

I continued to inform, and the mostly receptive class started asking questions.

The student who the teacher had to threaten away from the computer asked, "How much do you get paid?"

I turned to Dr. Morris and said, "Usually around 40 or 50,000 dollars to start, according to how big the university and what my responsibilities are. That's just to start." The students were not impressed. Then I asked a few volunteers to try on the robe. The regalia swallowed the children like a huge nightgown.

"Dr. Prevost, please come up and try on the regalia." She sheepishly walked into the robe that I held open for her. She made as many adjustments as necessary for a good fit. I asked Jarnee to walk like someone befitting the garb.

"Walk like a doctor."

Jarnee moved slowly with her thumb and index finger pinching her chin. She was a ham! After inspiring a few laughs from a captive audience, the bell rang. Most of the students stayed in their seats. At that moment I knew I wanted to work in New Orleans. A few hours later that day, I received a call and job offer from the dean.

Katrina Reunion

The officer moved a row of orange cones and pointed me to an uncongested parking area at the Monroe, La., shelter. After I parked my truck, I walked into the shelter through the closest doors. I found a back door to the theatre of operations. I stood in the rear of an open space filled with eight-foot long tables covered with white tablecloths. Evacuees moved aimlessly. But management had some kind of organization operating. Red Cross leaders tried to be as friendly as their drill-sergeant roles allowed. Too tired and confused, evacuees relied on the actions of the person in front of them. I knew it wouldn't be long before someone needed to find out where I belonged. I was lost. I noticed I didn't have a fluorescent green wristband. The lines, confusion and shock disturbed me.

After a year on the job as a professor, who would have thought I would be signing up for food and clothing vouchers from a Red Cross shelter. As I walked back to my truck, I noticed a young girl in a baggy Saints jersey and fitted denim capris crying on a green, metallic city bench about thirty feet away. A silver beret barely covered a bad perm, which looked like oily reeds of grass. Her cocoa-brown forearms resembled those of a child who'd spent a summer around a swimming pool. The sweat on her arms came from the 95-degree heat. But shrill infant cries came from her body. I wanted to help her. Her bright white Reeboks, which appeared too generic and new to be purchased, tapped the ground as she tried to calm the child. The chaotic setting camouflaged the baby's cries. Passers-by paid little attention. Before I could walk away, the girl sat up in her seat, uncovering the baby. The volume of the cries increased and the girl looked defeated. Then I recognized her face. I crept toward her, trying to buy the time to figure out how I knew her. I walked faster and my heart quickened. I thought to myself, could it be Dr. Prevost?

I said what I already knew, "Jarnee Prevost." She looked at me trying to remember. By the time she recognized me I stood directly over her. I asked, "Jarnee Prevost from Joseph Rainey?"

She shook her head in disbelief.

Desperate eyes flickered in her head.

I gave her a kiss on the cheek and sat next to her.

"How are you?" I asked.

She just looked at me and closed her eyes to hold back the tears left. I changed my question, "Where have you been?"

"Me and my baby have been riding this bus for three days." The baby's cries calmed for the moment.

"Where are your parents?"

"They're somewhere in Arkansas. I think a hotel."

"Who's with you?"

"Just my baby."

I could see that all of her possessions were stuffed in two baby bags, one blue, one pink; both appeared to have been given to her. Nonplussed, I asked, "How did you end up in Monroe? Why aren't you with your family?"

"I was staying with my boyfriend in the 10th Ward when the storm came. It didn't flood that bad, but we didn't have electricity or food. My baby only had enough formula till Wednesday. Then it just got crazy."

I could hear the desperation in her voice.

"People were going from house to house tying to get help. I saw them bustin' in people's houses when nobody answered the door.

"People were stealin' stuff. I was so scared for my baby girl."

"What's her name?"

"Talana."

"How old is she?"

"Six weeks." Her baby, covered with a diaper provided by the Red Cross, fell asleep during our conversation. The child's mocha skin was a warm contrast to the white loincloth. When Jarnee noticed Talana resting, it felt like a prayer answered.

Jarnee stared at Talana like a five-thousand piece jigsaw puzzle. After a few minutes of silence, I looked at Jarnee in the same way. A little more than a year ago she was responsible for learning the three branches of government. Now she learned how those branches didn't work in times of crisis.

"When was the last time you spoke to your family?"

"My brother Terry told me they were taken to Little Rock. My mom, brother and nieces and nephews were in the Superdome, but they made it out and ended up at the airport. They're flying a bunch of folks to safe places. I spoke to Terry yesterday, but his phone isn't working today. He probably ran out of minutes."

"Why weren't you with them?"

"Me and my mom aren't speaking over my boyfriend. She made us break up, but when she found out we were still dating, she kicked me out." Jarnee's simplistic story confused me.

"Why would she put you out?"

"He sold drugs." Like a guilty daughter to a wise father, Janee said, disgusted, "He tries to sell drugs."

I could tell she was done with defending him.

Jarnee replied with slight consternation, "Carrick is somewhere in New Orleans, and he doesn't want to be with us."

"We've got to get you help. You can't keep getting on buses moving from shelter to shelter. Your mama wouldn't let you and Talana live like this."

"My mom doesn't know my baby's name."

She looked down at Talana and continued, "I mean, my brother may have said something, but I never told her. She put me out." At that point the baby eked out the start of a long cry. Jarnee jerkily rocked the infant back to sleep.

"Listen Jarnee, I can take you to Little Rock."

"I'll just be in another shelter in Arkansas, Dr. Boyd." Jarnee started to cry, and I wanted to stop her tears. I cautiously massaged her shoulder to console her. She was all played out, rocking back and forth not to comfort the child, but herself.

I lost myself in her movement. While I rubbed the top of her back, she looked at me directly in the eyes and said, "Can you take Talana?"

Taken aback, I said, "You don't mean that."

Jarnee did not want words. She needed help. Jarnee knew she could not care for the child the way she wanted to or Talana needed. Deep inside I realized Jarnee believed this to be the most viable option. Sacrifice comes from love, and she loved her child. Still, I made feeble attempts to convince her otherwise.

"I will take you to Little Rock. Your family will help you find a way. When I take you there, I will make sure you have the services you need." Nothing worked. She kept asking me to take her child. She repeated, "When I get settled, I will come for her."

Before I could collect my thoughts, Jarnee placed Talana in

my arms.

"Please take her."

"I just can't take your child. There are laws and rules." I knew this was not completely true. I was informally adopted out of dire circumstances.

"I can't live like this."

"I don't have a home, either. I'm staying in a small room in my colleague's mother's house, and you want me to take a child. I'm not married and I barely have a job."

"You have more than I do."

"I'm sorry. I just can't. Let me get in touch with your parents. You can stay with my co-worker and me until you're settled."

With tears running off her chin, she took her child back and said, "I'll find my way."

7500 Teachers

November of 2005, I was among fewer than 90,000 people who returned to a city that had housed 450,000. Tree limbs punctured the roof of my Westbank home in several areas, requiring new shingles. Mold permeated walls in two rooms that needed new sheetrock, finishing and paint. My contractor used day laborers to complete these repairs and replace a few windows. Compared to 75 percent of the city that suffered flood damage, these were minor repairs.

The Westbank was "the best bank," in terms of recovery. With the addition of roaming National Guardsmen carrying machine guns and sprouting taquerias in the landscape, my neighborhood may have been livelier than before the storm.

Orleanians with means either got a head start or jumpstarted the recovery. The middle class returned in earnest, if not to stay, at least to assess damage. Teachers heard that schools on the Westbank formed an association to enroll many families whose homes suffered relatively little damage. Three of my teacher neighbors told us how encouraged they were that the School Board finally started opening public schools. In spite of better pay and working conditions, local educators did not get used to work and life elsewhere in the country. As we entered December, teachers moved back into the city and tried to secure jobs before an expected rush in January enrollment.

After a few days of conversations with a neighbor about her pending return to teaching, I overheard a TV news story that the board of New Orleans Public Schools considered firing most of its 7,500 workers at an evening meeting. I'd never heard of a system-wide mass firing. But the board, already burdened with debt, scandal and a negative reputation, did not have the money or power to rehire its employees. Therefore, the teachers received one paycheck on Sept. 1, after the storm. Thereafter, the bankrupt School Board placed all of its employees on administrative leave. Teachers held on to hope that they would be absorbed into reconstituted, smaller schools. But if reports were true, administrative leave would become official termination a few months later.

I knew a decision to summarily fire teachers would be one of the most pivotal moments in public education not only in New Orleans but nationwide. Teachers are a major political force in majority-black cities. Educators are the middle class. Where would my neighbors go? What would they do?

Teachers would not receive sympathy from those who had privileged seats at the recovery table. War rooms that organized the recovery did not seek to protect public school teachers.

Current and former teachers did not have the emotional or political support of public school families stuck in Houston, Atlanta, Baton Rouge and other cities. Public school families may not have economic or political strength individually, but collectively the working poor and working classes in New Orleans influenced how schools were managed. In their absence, change would be harsh and fast.

The storm blew wide open a political window of opportunity

to change educational infrastructure. Reformers sought to rearrange the hierarchy within school boards, unions, teacher groups, non-profits, policy and students. They wanted nothing less than a complete overhaul of public education.

Prior to the storm, New Orleans public schools had some of the worst educational outcomes in the country. The city also posted some of the worst health, incarceration and employment outcomes for African-Americans. A young boy could easily live in a St. Bernard public housing unit, go to Nelson Elementary where 99 percent of the students were eligible for free and reduced lunch, and later in the day go to the emergency room at Charity Hospital for health care where he could see one of his friends who was inadvertently shot in a family dispute.

Nevertheless, the potential of education is always spoken with violins playing in the background— as it should be. A quality education could transform lives like few other institutions. Because of this, teachers either become heroes or scapegoats. Even though there was blame to spare, the board's December actions would place it squarely in teachers' laps.

Somebody had to be accountable, but blame shouldn't be placed on the children. Good luck in holding parents or businesses responsible. Somebody had to feel the rage of people who managed public education by default.

When I arrived at the board meeting at McDonough 35 High School's auditorium, former employees of New Orleans Public Schools filled almost every seat. The typical cast of characters who attended every board meeting prior to the storm camped out in their regular sections. Black activists sat squarely in front of Board President Brendan Marshall. The white reformers sat in the back, to observe what they knew was coming. The multiracial coalition sat front, stage-left. I sat in the peanut gallery overlooking everything from the auditorium's balcony.

After stumbling through standing items, Marshall finally reached the reason why we were there. The preceding deliberations did not reveal what was to come. Marshall plainly said, "The NOPS Board will send an official notice of termination to all employees who have been placed on administrative leave." The crowd let out a gasp of disgust. The throng then fired verbal shots at the board. Marshall, an ordained minister, was not accustomed to this type of call and response. "You're a traitor!" "How could you?" "Fire the board!" "How can you live with yourself?" Marshall tried to calm the appropriately angry crowd.

He did his best to explain how the board could not open schools because it did not have funds or students. His repeated attempts to bring order almost incited a riot, which brought security to the dais. At that point, I feared for the board's safety. People began to press forward. The steady grumblings rose in volume like a threatening summer storm. I moved back toward the exit doors.

A local parent and teacher organizer recognized me as he walked around the periphery of the auditorium.

He asked, "Professor, what can be done? They just can't fire everyone. There has to be something we can do."

I could only reply, "I'm not sure."

The organizer shook his head as he contemplated the worst-case scenario.

Labor movements organize work because work organizes our lives. As a child, I remembered when U.S. Steel left Pittsburgh. Mom's husband's life soon followed. Pittsburghers believed that manliness was equated with manual labor. The only time we woke up to see my one father figure was Christmas. He wasn't supposed to walk us to school. Men were supposed to be working by that time.

Then came the economic drought. Teddy never got used to security work. We didn't understand his job loss either. The basis for my family's status and economic stability was farmed out to cheaper laborers in Europe. Within three years of losing his job in the mill, they said black lung killed Teddy. I thought whether my New Orleans neighbors would suffer similar fates.

The heart of black New Orleans was its teachers. I didn't want to witness more early deaths.

Just before I was about to leave I saw Dean Morris.

Dr. Morris said, "I don't know what we're going to do. The teachers we hired for the charter school are scattered across the country. So are the students." After kneading his forehead in frustration, Morris continued, "We have to open the school, but not even a third of our teachers are back."

I said, "Look on the bright side. You have lots of teachers to choose from, and they're available."

Morris chuckled, looked at the chaos and said, "You'd hire these folks? They're never going to get over this."

I said, "I don't think we have a choice."

Morris looked at the reformists who sat calmly in their seats while everyone else in the auditorium stood.

"We're going to have *choices* soon." The irony in his voice stung. He continued, "You don't think they're plotting to get The Teacher Plus Program and Teach for America down here?"

Morris knew New Orleans would have to rely on non-profits and charter schools to teach students already in New Orleans and for those who would be returning. Since charter schools have the autonomy to hire and fire their own personnel, an expansion of these school types would open doors for national teacher programs to take over in the unstable educational terrain of New Orleans. When reformers proudly said as a fundraising slogan, 'We have an opportunity to wipe the slate clean,' the elimination of local teachers was a possibly unintended but definitely real consequence. Also, the dean could see the threat to the local university providers. Charter schools did not have to hire local education graduates. It was not only teachers who would be blamed — local universities were also assumed to be responsible for hurting their own. Savior stories were primed to be the cure for New Orleans.

Then the dean looked at me sadly but positively as he said, "Isaac, you know I've had some health problems."

I'd heard he'd had some struggle with cancer, but I kept it to myself.

"This board meeting reminds me of the fights we faced when opening our charter school. The stress I suffered in the battle to open Johnson High wore me down. I don't think I can do it again."

My thoughts drifted to my neighbors. What would they do? Where would they go— thousands of people without jobs.

I turned to the Dean and said, "Whoever runs these schools will feel the pain of this meeting for years to come." The grumbling continued to bounce off the walls.

The dean said, "We're in a new era. The university needs new blood, new perspectives. This is a good time for me to bow out." I could hear wheels turning in his head.

"I've never seen New Orleans embrace an outsider like they've embraced you. Everyone likes you."

"Some dislike me as well. But thank you." He caught me by surprise. Until now, his recognition never rose beyond perfunctory hellos in the hallways.

"The city could use someone everyone can trust. New Orleans

needs a black leader."

I was always leery of white peoples' claims of the need for black leadership. The city was ripe for token leaders. The New Orleans school system needed a transformational leader regardless of race. When whites ordain leadership they give themselves credit for a successful selection and cast blame on failures. After erasing the blackboard, it becomes too easy for white architects to accept the roles of savior, sergeant and business person, while black educational leaders took on roles of preacher, social worker and activist. Still, I knew Morris saw the longterm need for communities to build up networks to run their own schools. Seventy-five percent of public school employees were black, so black aspirants and role models were critical keys to self-sufficiency.

Without its teachers, families and principals present, elected officials could more easily influence the fate of New Orleans public schools. Firing teachers could lock out the black middle class from deliberating in the recovery as much as boarding up public housing could with its residents. Diversity would take a back seat to "excellence" and "innovation." The 'no excuses' philosophy of new age reform has no patience for it. Educators have always struggled to see that diversity and inclusion are requisites of quality.

The anger had cooled as the crowd filed outside. But the reformers remained seated— too pleased and scared to move. With no intention of breaking down walls between private, parochial and public schools, the architects would not consider sending their children to schools they wanted to deconstruct. The black community would have to decide whether or not to take advantage of the coming changes. Fighting for a system that contributed to the man-made disaster did not make sense.

Fighting to run schools differently could be a cause célèbre. The charter banner that reformers used for their movement didn't worry me. Control of institutions is a pillar of self-determination. I felt the need to have greater control of my destiny— my schools. That attracted me.

Morris continued, "I need you to get our schools open and running."

I said, "I've never been a teacher or a principal. I'm a policy person."

"We need someone who can get us at the table. We're not players." Our place at the back of the bus proved his statement. Tulane University President Bruce Argence presided over the education committee of the Restore New Orleans Commission. Non-profits such as School Horizons already courted market- and charter-minded foundations. While the university was the first to acquire a charter school under the takeover legislation of 2004, we did not have influence on how the new system was being shaped. The dean wanted that power. I thought about the types of programs I'd always dreamed of placing in inner-city schools: debate teams, ethics courses, cross-country, jazz ensembles. I could make those programs happen, and I could definitely get us at the table.

The dean uttered what I could feel was coming when he said, "I would like you to head our efforts to run the charters."

"Wow."

I wouldn't downplay my abilities or desire that I wanted in, but I was speechless.

He said, "I'm going out of town for a week. Draft a brief job description for me so we can discuss it next week."

"Sounds like a plan."

"Good. And remember, it's *your* plan."

Structure

Change hurts. An education professor in urban schools feels like a capitalist in Cuba. As the new associate dean and CEO of the University of New Orleans Charter Network, I learned that university ideals don't hold water in urban school district culture. The labyrinth of public education rules is arcane— unless of course you are one of its architects. After only a few weeks of exploring the history and applicability of some of the idiosyncratic laws that lined the policy books, I learned its gatekeepers must cut deals with the devil. The adherence to rules and structure was nearly idolatrous. I must have heard the chant, "You can't do that," dozens of times when seeking practical solutions to streamlining financial reports or changing the school calendar. I tried using my rank and titles to appeal to their egos. My Ph.D. carried no weight in the state department. It may have been a liability. The assumption was that I was an idealist with no sense of reality.

"You've never been a teacher."

"You've never been a principal."

I was also labeled a charter-school pariah. Most times I succumbed to the gods of guidelines. However, my expeditions into bureaucracy gave me an idea why our schools were so strangled in red tape.

At the school level, structure, no matter how flimsy or wrongheaded, is the ostensible standard of a working school. For decades, how well a school adhered to district and state guidelines kept organizational charts and jobs in place, no matter how students performed educationally. Of course, the budget demanded the most strictures. Deficits were more likely to inspire radical change than negative student outcomes. Schools could fail thousands of children before making one structural change. However, if a budget shortfall was in the offing, change occurred immediately to balance it. Money, not students, drove the system.

The first few months on the job felt like a perpetual meeting: staff meetings, board meetings, teacher meetings, parent meetings, district meetings, behind-the-scenes meetings. But I attended few meetings that challenged old meeting behavior. I naively thought meetings were strictly about communication, planning, and decision-making. Meetings also solidified and reminded people of hierarchy. People didn't want changes in rank. There seemed to be a magic 60-minute allotment for each. No matter how detailed the topic, we had to rush or meander through an hour to set the next meeting. Comparatively speaking, at the university, it might take three hours to discuss a menu for the "end of semester" party. The culture of structure is so pervasive in public schools that employees demand meetings even when you work in the same building, talk five times a day, share meals and see each other at the daiquiri shop after work. Again, structure trumps performance. I was the anti-meeting CEO, which made no sense to employees. If you don't meet five times a day, you're not a leader. What I learned is that meetings are only as good as their products. I'd rather gather people ad hoc to solve problems.

This was seen as disorganized, or even lazy. But my goal was to knock down this rigid structure.

Even parents wanted it. In one of my first meetings with parents, 90 percent of the questions revolved around uniforms. When I said that I was not a fan of uniforms, you would think I'd said 'no homework,' which is an actual theory.

One parent said, "I don't want my child to compete with the next kid to have the most fashionable tennis shoes."

I retorted, "Good teachers will discourage that kind of materialism."

A mother said, "You don't know New Orleans. These kids shoot kids for Jordans," she said mentioning the pricey, popular tennis shoe.

I came back with, "Hopefully, students who are part of this school will understand the consequences of both wearing inappropriate clothing and stealing."

The woman finished with, "It's the kids who don't go to school that I worry about."

"Remember, you don't have to buy your child expensive clothes. Children don't purchase Jordans at Wal-Mart. They're getting these Jordans from their parents. As soon as your children get off a bus, a streetcar or wherever, they're targets. School should teach students the skills to handle these situations inside and out of school."

The parents nodded in agreement and a harmonious 'umm-hmm' buzzed through the auditorium.

"If the teachers can't give students the coping skills they need, then we need to find someone who will."

A parent in the front said loudly, "All right now."

Dozens more applauded.

I continued, "Ultimately, it's up to the principal, but at some point we've got to learn to trust children to be responsible. There are many other ways besides uniforms to enforce discipline."

One angry father stood and said, "I don't want to send my child to a place where the students can wear anything."

I said calmly, "Oh, we'll have a dress code, and it will be enforced. Students are in uniforms inside and outside of school every day. In public school, uniforms haven't curbed violence any more than higher incarceration rates have in the real world. Out of school, what would males wear without white tees and khakis? Our kids wear more uniforms than the military, but they are certainly not well disciplined."

After turning the room toward being more open to the possibility of a dress code, another "structural" issue emerged.

One parent stood and said, "There should be a ban on gift-giving in the school." I was dumbfounded.

I asked, "Why would you want to ban gift-giving?"

"On birthdays these kids be bringing big balloons, stuffed animals and all. It's a cost some kids can't meet." Suddenly, dozens of parents voiced their opposition to gifting. I could not believe this was such a volatile issue.

I could sense that the crowd at least wanted one hard, rule in place. The buzz grew to a rumble.

I stood, "One of my favorite days in high school was Fridays because the cheerleaders and my classmates would decorate my locker before a big game or race. Likewise, we showed people love by giving carnations and candy for important events. Our business club even sold the gifts. Something just doesn't sound right about a ban on gift-giving."

A woman rose, "They compete with each other and show off."

"Again, good teachers instill simpler principles of appreciation. As students develop, they know how to give and accept appropriate gifts."

Another parent stood and said, "They can give gifts, but only after school."

The crowd said, "That's good. That'll work."

I just shook my head and questioned privately why so many people essentially wanted schools mimicking something between a military academy and a prison.

But it was a citywide phenomenon. School leaders openly touted systems of discipline and order. It became matter-of-fact to say how inner-city students lacked discipline and order, and the quickest means to that were strict codes of silence or a speak-when-spoken-to-policy. From kindergarten to high school, the desire for this strange brand of discipline was universal. For me, discipline meant playing the cello every day after school or completing assignments or not being truant. Discipline never meant literally toeing a line in a school library. Nevertheless, teachers, parents and principals alike supported this paradigm, and this mimicked schools' meeting models.

To understand the new educational landscape, I toured the best of the new charter and traditional schools. Both types with low-income students demanded uniforms and all the hegemony that comes with them. Given a choice, the only schools without uniforms were those with middle-class students.

Charter and traditional schools emphasized how orderly their educational spaces were. I found them to be painfully quiet and glaringly robotic. The teachers I interviewed viewed quality classroom management as a controlled environment where students "knew the consequences of their behavior." Also from primary to secondary, I noticed that teachers creatively delivered a "banking" model of instruction in which facts were deposited into children's learning accounts. The constant drilling of information certainly fit into the highly structured environment I'd encountered. It also meshed well with standardized testing. However, what happened to the disorganized noise that goes on in children's heads? Where was the questioning of the information and teachers? Teachers constantly praised their school leaders for instilling order and discipline. They would say that students have no structure in their homes, and schools needed to fill the void. What happened to schools being schools and parents being parents?

There was something horribly stifling about this. It restricted the amount of questions that could be raised. School leaders became accustomed to visitors gladly stating how quiet and organized their buildings were. I asked if anyone was in the building, but I wasn't supposed to question the structure. Order and efficiency ran schools. Questioning was an inefficient noise that got in the way of "learning." Consequently, "questioning" rarely existed in the schools' cultural or academic vocabulary. Schoolboys and girls could not question God, parents, teachers or any grown-ups. No matter how incongruent the world seemed inside or outside those classrooms, children were told not to question. Educators, families and boosters all bought into this idea of structure.

To silence children's questions, elders sternly said "listen." Before a child could ask a question, they would hear from parents, teachers, and preachers, 'Boy, would you listen?' or 'If you didn't talk so much, maybe you could learn something.' Students likened listening to silence, silence to obedience, and obedience to survival. Schools' social organizations considered noise a sign of transgression.

Ironically, in the birthplace of jazz, Orleanians relied on structure the same as gravity. We didn't want different schools.

We wanted what we believed to be Catholic schools. We wanted ruler-swatting nuns in control. This might work for a privileged few. However, disenfranchised folk needed to learn how to question and raise their voices. What I saw was that reformers wanted students to fear authority instead of understand it. Understanding what happened after Hurricane Katrina would make one want to "holla." Given a chance to create a new music, I was hearing the same old dirge— poor kids need to be controlled.

Mr. Simon Will Save Us

It didn't take long to discover the hydra of the reform movement. My pre-storm media exposure gave me credibility and a leg up on the competition. I had the freedom to chide new-age white reformers and push unsympathetically on predominantly black schools, policy makers and leaders. In spite of my position and dominion, I definitely didn't have the strength to dam the evangelistic tide of the charter schools movement. Their version of the heaven or hell altar call went something like, 'You can have the former system, or you can have an opportunity.' For parents, businesses and private school families, believing in school reform became practically a religion. Charter leaders' *with us or against change* ideologies yielded foundation and private giving as well as media exposure. Those who were *with* received the bounty. Those *against* received tongue lashings.

Post-storm policy washed away the system's former teachers and leaders with the rest of the hurricane debris. A few months after the firings, a defunct School Board did not renew the union's collective bargaining agreement, which gave charter school leaders more freedom to hire and fire "their own" teachers.

The new charter schools seemed to have an unwritten policy not to hire former New Orleans teachers. Many leaders chose to hire a new crop. The majority of my employees were former Orleans Parish, traditionally-trained educators. Therefore, I became a questionable member of the movement. I aimed to hire local stars. However, finding talented teachers and principals proved difficult, as the most talented were settling elsewhere. Also, I did not want to hear, "This is how we used to do it before." I needed effective local teachers and principals who could forge new paths. I consequently fired our original principal and dozens of teachers. However, the rehires didn't change racial percentages or the balance of local teachers.

During our teacher and leader search for the summer of 2006, I was introduced to Mr. Simon from New Orleans. Schools had only been open for six months and Simon was a twice-fired charter school teacher. Flood waters destroyed his personal and family homes. Simon lived in a trailer while he worked on his Ph.D. in educational leadership, and he worked full time. After teaching in Alabama until the January after the storm, Simon landed a charter school job with Crescent City Prep in the Ninth Ward. That job did not last long as he argued with the school's founder, Principal Brian Rice, about discipline. Students wore "Not Yet" signs on their backs if they didn't demonstrate appropriate learning behaviors. Students were forced to walk up and down stairs as punishment if they talked in the hallways. When Simon complained, Rice reminded him that the state of Louisiana permits corporal punishment. Leadership also expelled several students with combative and explosive behaviors. These students eventually enrolled in the takeover school district named the Recovery School District. Mr. Simon held on to the idea that public education was a right that must be protected. He also held on to the notion that not everything was wrong with the former system. And he questioned. He asked, "*Why?*" Mr. Simon's questioning was perceived as defiance and insubordination. Simon was counseled out for the good of culture building. Simon would be fired from another charter school for similar reasons.

In spite of his recent record, Simon interviewed well. He was 35, energetic and possessed an edge that I couldn't fathom. New Orleanians have a peculiar persona that stems back to Plessy v. Ferguson and Reconstruction. He didn't have a chip on his shoulder. Simon was principled. This filled my profile of desirable black males who defied stereotypes. He projected this in his interview. We hired him for our takeover high school, Lyndon Johnson. Because the flood destroyed more than 70 percent of the school stock, including the original Lyndon Johnson site, schools cohabitated in buildings until permanent facilities were found. As irony would have it, the state requested our high school share a building with one of the charter schools that fired Mr. Simon, Crescent City Prep. Johnson and Crescent were both housed in the disbanded Joseph Rainey High School building.

* * *

As part of the school and teacher evaluation process, I randomly observed teachers in action. After serving a few months in the classroom, Mr. Simon's positive reputation preceded him. I decided to visit his ninth-grade civics class for one week. During that time, I keyed in on a special relationship Mr. Simon had with a ninth-grader named Loren Wise. I could see that Loren fooled everyone else into thinking he was the coolest nerd in school. He wore a raggedy afro that might work into dreads. He would twist his baby-fro when he was nervous. I liked that Mr. Simon recognized that Loren's pimp strut was actually a limp.

He was busted. The rest of Loren's teachers mistook his irregular gait for swagger. But Simon told no one what he knew.

Before the storm Loren lived with his parents in the 9th Ward, but his school record showed he had seven different addresses up to the months after the breaches in the levees. Loren's latest address was three blocks away from Mr. Simon in the Upper Nine. In fact, Mr. Simon often drove Loren to school. In spite of his transient existence, Loren excelled in school. He had posted perfect attendance since the first grade. His verbal skills did not match his language arts test scores, which placed him at advanced levels, and he only approached basic scores in math, but he generally tested higher than his peers. He did not like the hostile and crass students, but school became his sanctuary.

However, during the last school semester before the storm, his father came to a parent-teacher conference to discuss a fight Loren got into. The teacher did not suspend the students, but let the parents know. The teacher informed his father, who didn't live with Loren and his mother. After a one-on-one with the teacher, Loren's father entered the room at the start of class and asked Loren to apologize to his classmates. While he offered an apology, his father pulled off his belt and proceeded to whip Loren. The teacher tried to intervene but a fierce stare made her call security. When security arrived in less than a minute, the officer restrained his father, then police arrested him. Despite the incident, Loren came back to school the next day, though students mimicked the beating whenever they caught Loren's eye. The aftermath of Katrina paled in comparison to the storm raging inside Loren. With his father in Houston with his siblings, Johnson High School offered Loren a new start.

"OK class, are you ready for your examination on the presidential and vice-presidential election process?" Simon asked with gusto.

The rowdy group of ninth-graders yelled a resounding, "Yes," that echoed through the halls. This was typical of Mr. Simon's classes. Room 104 was hardly sedate. Loren's favorite teacher proudly conducted the class and reveled in his ability to stir up excitement. Mr. Simon ignored the rigid style of teachers in Johnson and Crescent City Prep Charter Schools. Mr. Simon's peers equated student vocalization with delinquency. Prep teachers from down the hall and the floor beneath frequently interrupted with requests for quiet. Not only did Mr. Simon receive visits from Prep, but also Johnson teachers came by, delivered their appeals and walked away. The class giggled when petitioners exited.

Simon's students' reactions indicated the respect they held for him. The kids were as proud of Mr. Simon as he was of them, and he was appreciative. Simon was one of the few teachers who allowed students to have a voice. Other teachers thought they were doing me a favor by asking me to spend additional time in Mr. Simon's class to hear how loud and unruly students behaved. I obliged and continued my observation. However, his teaching style invigorated my visits and gave me a break from the administrative doldrums.

Students who Mr. Simon taught were proud and self-assured. Simon's students, as he put it, were "curiously confident and confident of their curiosity." From the moment they set foot in his class, they were encouraged to question. His creative use of pictures, artifacts, and readings turned the classroom into one that primed his students for the real world. His room reflected eras, aesthetics, architecture, and sensibilities of the periods they studied. Simon immersed students in lessons. His pedagogical style was outside the box and revolutionary compared to how other teachers taught.

Selection Thursday in Room 104 marked the most significant day in Loren's political life. It was part of the month-long unit on the election process in American Civics. Simon's classes often shadowed contemporary community issues. For instance, during his investigation of the federal government, Simon invited each candidate from the second district congressional race to teach a lesson on the three branches of government. He called it the "Substitute Teacher Challenge." Many of the candidates hadn't stepped foot in a public school in years. Simon wanted them exposed to street-level post-Katrina issues. Simon gave the students teacher evaluations at the end of each candidate's class. The highest evaluation merited an endorsement from the school.

As soon as the media caught wind of the substitute teacher challenge, the politicos were attracted to the lights of the camera. With a captive audience, Simon planted specific questions that addressed deplorable conditions of the facilities as well as national legislation to insert creationism or intelligent design in science textbooks. One student asked a Republican candidate, "What's the role of the church if they're trying to teach creationism in public schools?" Another asked the Democratic incumbent, "What legislation have you supported to rebuild American school facilities?" With cameras rolling, students unashamedly threw inquiries that conventional debates didn't care to broach.

This week the task focused on presidential candidates. Actual elections were days away, and students were to demonstrate mastery of the electoral process. The class blasted through fundraising, campaigning, lobbying, the Electoral College, and acceptance speeches. Through intense deliberations and politicking, students would select the next class president.

I made a point to attend selection Thursday. Mr. Simon

passed around a bag of destinies in the form of little white pieces of paper. Each slip described a stakeholder's wardrobe that must be imitated precisely. The image students were to project provided motivation in the presidential drama. Everyone in class had an agenda, but collective decisions affected goals. The class understood the aim wasn't to memorize election rules. Simon challenged students to understand why and how stakeholders advanced agendas. The test lay in students' abilities to articulate and manipulate perspective and position, dominance and vulnerability, leadership and responsibility.

Red, white, and blue banners festooned the classroom. In the beginning of the week, Simon positioned students evenly in the double arches in the center of the room; however, by its end, Mr. Simon's democratic process tilted the players towards the left. The overcrowded room gave little opportunity to engage in much political maneuvering. The pictures of donkeys and elephants provided polar distinctions along a political axis. During these days, students stared at two vacant podiums representing the debates for president. Students tried the podiums on for size and gave extemporaneous speeches to get a feel for the contest.

On this selection Thursday, as soon as Simon made the satin, black bag visible, all joking ceased. An anxious silence swept through the room as the resonant voice of Mr. Simon took over.

"There are forty-two leaders in the class. I will ask each of us to take a position and role of profound influence. Our future is at stake. How you participate in the future is of extreme importance. I trust that you have gained enough information throughout the term on the political process. How will you act on that information? Once every four years, *some* citizens have opportunities to perform real symbolic gestures of extreme importance. Determining the president of the United States is much more involved than placing ballots in a box or choosing candidates of certain political affiliations.

"As you know, you must *question*..."

The students chimed in on cue, "... the actors, goals, motivations, resources, strategies, settings, and interactions."

Mr. Simon continued, "Your grade will not only reflect your ability to memorize roles of individual actors in the election process. Although that is important, you must learn the dynamic political process as a whole.

"There are forty-two characters in the bag. Forty-two slips of paper could never encapsulate the variety of determinants in a presidential election. You will be graded on your ability to see your position in relation to millions of others nationwide. Imagine the impact of your voice. Learn how to amplify your voice. Learn how others suppress your voice. Learn that you have choices. Voting is not the only way to impact change. Choices made before the election have significant impact on its outcome and your futures. Once you know you have choices, you are responsible for making more. When you leave this classroom, you have enough information to ask questions, find definitive answers, and take positions on your future. Do you want that responsibility?"

The class responded in unison, "Yes."

"Then let's begin."

The class took a deep breath as Mr. Simon walked toward the first student. He asked her to dig in the bag. Mr. Simon then reached in the bag, picked his own fortune, and wrote his name on the board beside the name of the character he would play in the electoral drama. The class respected Mr. Simon's knowledge on issues, and they hung on every word he wrote. Whatever he chose, the class knew Simon would be a formidable player.

Mr. Simon picked Charles Van Collins, CEO and President of a multinational corporation, American Eagle Media Group. Although the class did not explicitly express resignation, the looks they gave each other connoted concern.

I thought to myself, "He has the information and a big position, damn."

I am sure his students thought the same. Mr. Simon walked with a grin away from the student holding the bag. The class responded with a haughty chuckle and an air of confidence as if to say, "We are not afraid."

Mr. Simon motioned to pass the bag along to each student. One by one, students chose a role name and position and wrote them on the board. Silence continued throughout. Students meticulously wrote down names and positions. Some roles matched a student's personality and temperament. Others didn't. Students silently sized up the pairings.

Mr. Simon watched as the bag came to Katura and Loren. Katura reached in and walked silently to the board. Loren took a deep breath, and hoped for the best. Although he felt comfortable playing multiple roles, like everyone else, Loren wanted to be president. As the class learned throughout the term, the hype of the mythic position always exceeds the real role. The more the class demystified the role of president, the more Loren appreciated its significance. Although bound by party loyalty, public sentiment, money ties, check systems, and rigid ideology, the president performs on the world's largest stage. The possibilities were enormous.

You could see Loren thinking, "If I had the voice of the president, what would I do? What would I say?"

Before that particular class, all Loren cared about was Saints football, a few video games and the possibility of kissing Katura.

Now he considered other possibilities.

Loren's paper read, "Lee Ferguson, Democratic Presidential candidate." He rushed to the board in excitement only to find that Katura had picked "Tracy Green, Republican Presidential candidate." He read the complete descriptions of their characters.

Katura was the most polished student in class. She studied ferociously. Since Loren met Katura, he was always impressed with her level of discipline, commitment and passion for learning. Loren thought she probably developed that drive from her parents, who were very religious. Loren rarely went to church, but every time he attended, Katura sat in the front pew. He couldn't miss her. Katura's parents knew Loren's father, and they made extra efforts to keep a watchful eye over Loren, who they knew needed guidance. That's how Katura and Loren grew close. Katura's family invited Loren's mother over for dinner and various church events. As they got older, his older sister Danielle pressed Loren to be a boyfriend to Katura. He'd barely advanced beyond admiration, primarily because he was bowled over by Katura's skills, strength and attitude. Katura would not be disrespected, and if she was, the wrath of God was upon you. Loren learned from her that girls with goals didn't give themselves, bodies or souls, away.

No one was immune to Katura's intelligence. She was astute and demanding. If provoked, her pretty brown lips let loose a firestorm of biblical texts and attitude. She paid keen attention to details. With the exception of God and her parents, Katura submitted to no one. Like most students, she knew why teachers wanted silence. But unlike most, Katura challenged authority. Born with a preacher's tongue, Katura banished idiocies with eloquence and immaculate delivery. She damned racist, sexist and classist innuendos that teachers unconsciously spouted or explicitly stated. Katura kept everyone on their toes.

Running for president against Katura would also be difficult because everyone, including Loren, admired her. Katura protected him from the insidious social critiques of his teachers. Teachers regularly asked Loren and his classmates, "Do you read when you get home?" "You have too much potential to hang with those thugs." "We don't need any more athletes." Negative reinforcement was the dominant modus operandi. The faculty consistently criticized Loren's hair, clothes, speech and family as a way to motivate him. His peers shut out teachers instead of being belittled and refused to learn more than the bare minimum.

But Loren didn't ignore teachers' critiques. When the subjects got hard, he put in more work and time. Though Loren was too embarrassed to ask his teachers for help, Katura lent a hand. She helped Loren with math, science, English and music.

When the two started middle school, they would take daily trips to the library and review lessons. For almost a year, Loren did not really contribute to the sessions, but Katura didn't mind. She spoke Loren's language and she understood teachers. Katura translated abstractions into concrete information. He loved learning with Katura. Math quickly became his favorite subject. While Loren barely understood Mr. Horowitz's math lessons, Katura made them seem easy.

While she managed to rescue Loren's academics, her belief in him didn't parallel his teachers' beliefs. Many of Loren's days began with a reminder of his worth. His homeroom teacher, Ms. Hogan, grew up in the 9th Ward but moved to the affluent English Turn area when she married. Although she moved out of the community, she held on to the rights and privileges of a local. Generations were taught by Ms. Hogan and never questioned her style. Loren was an easy target. She ridiculed him daily. One day Ms. Hogan, disgusted by his appearance, sat him in a chair and started combing his hair.

During the violent raking of his scalp, Ms. Hogan mumbled, "These parents send their kids out the house looking any kind of way. They don't even comb their hair anymore. I don't know what's wrong with these folks." Loren's classmates often laughed. Luckily they'd escaped Hogan's wrath. Ms. Hogan seemed to take her frustration with many parents out on his tender head. Paralyzed by her imperiousness, he sat hopelessly through the drubbing. During one of the episodes, Katura saw that the pain in his face wasn't entirely due to the combing. She pulled him from the seat and yelled at Ms. Hogan.

"You're not his mother! As if you care about us!"

Katura's statement represented feelings Loren and his classmates would not express. Even though his peers laughed, they too had felt the brunt of Hogan's assumptions at some point in their school careers. Though she bothered others, Ms. Hogan never ridiculed Loren again.

* * *

After the class received its assignments, they started to think about their next moves. As Mr. Simon ended class, Mr. McClain, the ninth- and tenth-grade English teacher, conspicuously entered the class to observe. A thirty-year veteran, Terry McClain often complained about the class's noise. He settled in by the door and leaned against one of the elephants on the wall. Although McClain was an obese, dark-skinned man, the skepticism evident on his face was his most prominent feature. Typically, jeers and disdain welcomed McClain. However, the class was so focused on their activity they barely noticed him.

Mr. Simon stated with enthusiasm, "When you return tomorrow, I expect that you will be prepared to engage in a political discussion with your peers. Information pertinent to the election process will be placed on your desk when you return. Take this election seriously. Your two presidential candidates are counting on you."

Mr. Simon appeared pleased that Katura and Loren were selected.

He continued, "I have good news. Dr. Sarnacola has allowed all ninth-graders to vote. So you can campaign in every class."

The students cheered loudly. Katura and Loren looked at each other, mentally calculating the higher stakes.

Mr. Simon said, "See yourselves as president. It could happen." On cue, the bell sounded. The period's end left everyone with visions of a better future.

Katura and Loren walked to their next class. As they passed Mr. McClain, Katura stared at him. His brows furrowed and dared her to speak.

"I'll see you later Katura," said Mr. McClain.

Loren grabbed her arm and pulled her toward the doorway. The last student exited the room as Mr. Simon gathered himself at his desk.

"Clifford, what brings you my way," Mr. Simon said pleasantly.

"Hello Dr. Boyd. I hope you're capturing all this," McClain said.

I said, "I am. How are you?"

McClain interjected, "The constant noise from Mr. Simon's class is disruptive to the school."

Mr. Simon responded, "How many times in the last three months have I asked that you call me Malik?"

"Mr. Simon, do you realize that the state examinations are

approaching?"

Nonplussed, Mr. Simon exhaled a long, "Yeeesss."

Angered by Simon's nonchalance, McClain snapped, "Well, what are you doing?"

Simon responded calmly, "You should know what I'm doing. You were just watching my class."

"Do you think these tests are some type of game? These students' futures are at stake."

Before Katura and Loren reached their next class, Loren noticed he forgot his civics book. He hustled back to Mr. Simon's room dazed by the previous class. As he approached the room, he overheard adult voices and discreetly paused outside to listen.

Mr. Simon continued, "I do this exercise because I am keenly aware of what is at stake in these kids' lives."

"So why are you distracting them at a time when they should be preparing for the test?"

"I do not teach for a test. I teach for a lifetime of learning."

"Mr. Simon, would you get your head out of your ass and look around? Like it or not, we are in a system that rewards tests and testing. If they do not pass their exams, not only will they fail in life, we will lose what little autonomy we have left. I know you swim in your popularity, but your ego is hurting these kids."

Mr. Simon was beside himself, "Is that what you think? I am doing this to pump myself up? Let me tell you something, *Mr. McClain*. I want these kids to be able to correct a broken system, not add to the list of casualties."

"Correct how? You think *these* kids will someday be president? If you think these kids should dream about becoming president, you're crazy. You better pray they don't become felons so they can at least vote. We're in one of the poorest districts in the state. Even our best students are not shoo-ins for college. Fifty percent of them drop out. Ten percent go to college. Seventy-five percent of them don't have both parents in their home. Half of those parents are alcoholics or addicts."

McClain was on a roll.

"The best advice you could give your students is to tell them that white folks aren't going to let them be president. Hell, these whites aren't going to let them get a decent job. If they're lucky, they can get out of this hell-hole, go to community college, and work their way up. They simply need to stay out of trouble and avoid getting pregnant or shot!"

"Just because you've lost faith in these kids, doesn't mean I should." Mr. Simon was angry.

"I've been in New Orleans for more than thirty years and I've seen hundreds of young teachers like you, thinking they can change the world. Ultimately their fantasies of changing the world die and they leave the system. Almost all those teachers end up in Jefferson Parish or Catholic and private schools. Every year we get a new crop of naïve recruits who come in with their fancy curricular models and newfangled teaching. They *all* leave, *Mr. Simon*. I'll give you a few more years till you see your students on the street begging for a handout, and they won't recognize you. You'll barely recognize them. You'll change, too."

"I don't know about you Mr. McClain, but I grew up in the city. I had teachers who believed in me. Ms. Hogan drove me home every day because she lived next door. When my mother couldn't, Ms. Hogan fed me. When my family worked the night shift, she made sure I got breakfast and to school. You can hide in your house in New Orleans East and give up because so many of these children have failed. I have to go home to the same house I was raised in, in the same block Loren lives in, the same block you left, Mr. McClain."

Mr. McClain had to have been insulted because his home received over 12 feet of floodwater. "Loren has as much a chance of becoming president of France as he does of being president of the United States. I would have more respect for you if you told him the truth."

"And what's the truth, McClain?"

"Black kids can't dream so big." Mr. McClain drew closer to Mr. Simon. "You better take your MLK dreams to some other district. Do you know where Loren's father is, Mr. Simon?

"I don't," Mr. Simon said.

"Neither does this school, his mother nor Loren. All we know is that he lives with his abused mom who left her girls in Houston. Loren is a poor, black male from the 9th Ward. He is a smart kid, enveloped in a set of circumstances no school can save him from. We need to get Loren ready for the state exams and get him out of this school."

Mr. Simon responded, "What about after graduation, Mr. McClain? What then? Sure he'll pass the exams, but what did he learn?"

Cutting Mr. Simon short, McClain said, "You act like doing well in this school might get students somewhere. You think a charter is going to change the fact he will be a New Orleans public school graduate? Orleans is an academic scar. Colleges don't want kids from here. Employers don't hire our graduates. Communities fear students from this school. Tell Loren to get as far away from this place as possible, and that a good test score can help him."

"A good education will give Loren the power to choose where he wants to go. A good test score will push Loren where society wants him to go, away from his people."

"The Black Star Movement died with Marcus Garvey."

"Don't disrespect me, Mr. McClain. Loren needs to learn and believe that there are those who are truly committed to ensuring that his community empowers itself to shape its own destiny."

"What destiny is that, Mr. Simon?"

"The destiny the community chooses, Mr. McClain."

At that point a deep voice bellowed from the end of the hallway. "Loren, aren't you supposed to be in class? Where's your pass?" Mr. McClain and Mr. Simon looked towards the door as Loren entered the classroom. He went back to the room to retrieve a forgotten bookbag.

Loren asked sheepishly, "Can I have a pass, Mr. Simon?"

McClain suspected Loren had heard the conversation and looked pleased.

"Sure you can have a pass."

Mr. Simon silently signed the yellow sheet of paper. "Here you go. Hurry up to class." Without looking up or speaking a word, Loren walked over to Mr. Simon and slowly reached for the pass. Mr. Simon grabbed his wrist for a brief moment then placed the pass in his hand.

McClain firmly stated, "Hurry up now. Your teacher is waiting for you."

Loren slowly looked up and deep into McClain's eyes for a long time. Simon then grabbed his shoulders and pointed Loren toward the door. Loren limped out of the class with a disdain of standardized tests in his head and belly and an even greater contempt for Mr. McClain.

Running to School

If you can't stand the heat, stay out of the kitchen. Ms. Wise constantly used this expression as a motivational tool. Of course she meant endure the struggle. However, did she really understand what that meant?

Every day after school, Loren loped into the kitchen to see what his Mom had cooked for dinner. Rena Wise took the opportunity to talk with him about schoolwork and social life. Rena stood between the beans and rice so she caught his attention. The daily interrogation was pleasant or painful, depending on Loren's situation. Loren knew he had to report not only to eat, but also to satisfy his mother. She missed talking to Loren's sisters, so she poured all her attention onto Loren. He didn't mind talking. Ms. Wise always gave sound advice. However, after a long, hard day of politicking, Loren's kitchen time was a relief, and he didn't look forward to additional demands.

"How was your day, Loren?"

His mom's question seemed more pointed than usual.

Loren replied half-heartedly, "OK."

He was not OK. The first phase of the election inundated him with a deluge of information and chaos. Doubts raced through his head.

He wondered why he wanted the presidency. Loren anticipated the outcome with excitement, but was staggered by the work and pressure. He felt an emotional tug of war. There was no place he'd rather be, but he sought excuses to bail out.

Running against Katura was exhausting. How could he really best her? Intellectually and socially, he needed to win to heighten his status at school. This was his neighborhood Super Bowl. If he won, he could have hood immunity from its chaos and physical confrontations. With so much at stake, emotionally, he was unprepared. The hill of an election is a long climb, and Loren made camp halfway up.

But he developed an even greater appreciation of Katura. He could not believe how calm she seemed during the process. Not only did she advance her platform, she still helped Loren pull his classes together. He cherished her assistance but wondered if he could do it on his own.

The more they studied together, the more Loren realized his shortcomings. Katura reminded him of what he missed in school. Loren hurt thinking of running against the person he relied upon. The pressure was on, and he had only a few days before the election.

"Have a seat, Loren." He pulled up a chair from beneath the wooden counter that served as a dining and conference table. He sat on the edge of the seat. His mom leaned against the sink. He saw that she'd almost finished putting away the leftovers. A last plate waited on the gas stove.

"Guess who paid me a visit, Loren?"

Loren usually had the ability to decipher his mom's intent. The slightest change of pitch could mean the difference between praise and putdown. But he had no idea who'd come by, so he was silent.

"You know Dr. Sarnacola?" she asked.

"Yes, ma'am," he said nervously, wondering why his principal would visit.

"He tells me you've been late to school."

She paused, and examined Loren's face, looking for answers. He'd never been late or a liar. "When Dr. Sarnacola told me how many times you were late this semester, I thought, how could Loren be late if he gets on the bus every day? So I asked him, 'How can that be, Dr. Sarnacola? I watch him get on the bus.' You know what he told me?"

"I don't get off the bus stop with the other kids."

"Excuse me?"

Loren said, "I get off the city bus early and walk."

Irritated, she asked, "Loren DaShaun Wise, you'd better explain!"

"I'm tired of riding the bus. The kids mess with people."

"Who messes with you?"

"I don't know— everybody."

"You don't know? That doesn't sound right, Loren."

"What I meant to say was that the *Fiya Boyz* get on the bus and ask for people's money."

"Why can't you do anything about it? Go to your teachers, and tell them who's picking on you. I'll call the police."

"Then I'll be a snitch."

"Let me get this straight. You'd rather get robbed than be a snitch. You'd rather get punished by me and put up with bullies? I thought I taught you better. Besides, why are you letting some bullies pick on you?"

"I'm not scared."

At that moment, a rush of embarrassment prickled over Loren's skin. He knew that he was running away from his problems but was too ashamed to admit it. He also knew that his mother had run away from her problems to no avail.

Males have a code. Defeat is tolerable. Losing a fight is acceptable. Avoiding confrontation, on the other hand, is unacceptable and cowardly in the hood. Although most boys on the bus were similarly bullied, hood laws prohibited acknowledging fear. He couldn't admit this to his mother without feeling like less of a man. He also did not want to reopen her old wounds.

"I don't want to get on the bus," he said.

"If you're scared, then tell me."

"I'm not. I just don't want to ride the bus."

"Didn't I teach you to stand up for yourself?"

"I'm tired of being pushed around. I can't fight like the other boys with this leg and they know it."

"Boy, you think fighting is the only way to stand up for yourself? You have to use other ways."

His mom was old school. Loren looked at her skeptically. Even though Loren knew that she, like other young mothers on the block, encouraged her child to stand up for himself and his family, Rena's speeches dismissed his very real fears. The adage of *stand up to the bully* and eventually good will triumph over evil was a simplistic and dangerous treatment of Loren's situation. Avoiding confrontation was impossible in New Orleans. Fighting was a given, and fighting begot fighting. If you did not fight, you welcomed antagonism from those who did, which led to more fighting. No matter the method, hiding in fear was futile. Loren in particular tried to use wit to daze his antagonists. But Loren's verbal jabs were an ineffective means of coping. His mom knew what he faced, but Loren wondered why couldn't she accept what he felt. He was trying to find a way to cope.

Loren erupted, "I don't want to ride that bus. I'll be late."

He spoke angrily and loud. Ms. Wise turned her head sideways and looked him down from head to toe.

He squeaked out, "You never stood up to Dad."

Rena took a step back. She gritted her teeth and redirected the conversation.

"So you get off the bus early and get to school late every day?"

"I'll get up earlier so I can get to school on time."

"You are missing the point, Loren DaShaun. Dr. Sarnacola and I are worried about your safety. The school is four miles away. Something may happen to you."

"It's safer to go the way I take."

"You're avoiding the issues."

"Please don't make me go on the bus."

Ms. Wise then gave a stern and sudden reply, "You will stay on that bus, and you won't let those bullies win. I am going to tell Dr. Sarnacola. You have to stay on that bus."

She caught herself sounding desperate and changed her tone. After her declaration, Loren attempted another angle.

"Mom, I am really trying hard in school."

Ms. Wise allowed the digression. "Dr. Sarnacola told me your schoolwork has improved."

"Before I got by. Now I really want to learn. I need to get serious, but what happens on the bus in the morning ruins my day. Mom, I can't get beat up by those boys every morning. You ought to know how that feels. I didn't want to mention Dad. I'm glad he's gone. It's the same thing."

Ms. Wise looked at him sadly and kneeled next to his chair. His head dropped onto her shoulder.

"You're scared. I'm scared, too. Parents have no idea what is going on in those buses. We don't have a clue what's going on in classrooms. When I grew up, we fought and were friends the next day. My friends teased me, but it didn't amount to much. On the other hand, we didn't center our lives on school. That didn't mean I didn't learn. I have a 10th-grade education, but I read all the time. And I earned my GED.

"At this point in my life, I care more about your education and safety. There is nothing anyone can do that will take away what we have."

With one hand she grabbed Loren's right hand, which rested on the table. With her other she lifted his head so she could look into his eyes. Gently she placed her palm on his cheek.

"I am so proud of you, Loren. Dr. Sarnacola told me that he has seen changes in your attitude. He believes you are going to be elected president of your ninth-grade civics class."

Rena's smile erased some fear from his heart. Loren's eyes moved back to the table.

"Do you want to be President Loren?"

He replied with a small, "Yeah."

She paused and looked at him for a few seconds, from his weak leg to his strong face. He had some constitution, she thought.

"All right then, you have a deal."

Loren looked in her face incredulously.

She continued. "I will call the school and tell them you will take another bus. But, you're going to arrive ON TIME."

Loren's mouth fell open. In the past, he was never able to compromise with his mom.

"But…"

Loren knew there was a catch.

"If you are going to run away from your problems then you might as well strengthen that weak leg."

"What do you mean?"

"You have to run after school every day."

"Run after school? How far?"

"Two miles."

"I don't have the shoes."

"We will go to the mall this weekend to get you some running shoes."

"Are you serious?"

"I'll call your physical therapist to see that it's OK. If they approve, it's done. If not, then you have to do physical therapy to get that leg stronger. I thought you were tired of folks messing with you.

"I am giving you an opportunity to face your foes. You can't beat that." Before he could get the look of bewilderment off his face, she said, "Before you make your decision there are some conditions.

"If you are late to school, then you have to return to the old bus and the old bullies. If your grades drop, then you have to get back on the old bus. Also, you have to call me on a phone every day from the principal's office to let me know that you've arrived safely and on time to school." She paused while he thought.

"Is it a deal?"

Loren thought, if you can't stand the heat, get out of the kitchen. He wondered if he could keep his end of the bargain, but said, "Deal!"

The Uptown Crowd

It was my first meeting with the "Uptown" reform crowd hosted by community dignitary and socialite Pearly du Bourg. Her palatial 19th century French neoclassical home epitomized the term bourgeoisie. The section of town upriver from the French Quarter is one of the most diverse areas of the city. However, distinct images of sazeracs, seersucker suits, black servants and old homes immediately come to mind in the scuttlebutt about the Uptown reform crowd.

As an outsider, I was always taken aback at how flimsy neighborhood identities seemed to be. In order to get to Pearly's home I passed blacks and whites in dreadlocks, hot boy bike riders and neutral-ground drunks. However, the separation of a few city blocks made me realize the invisible divide between blue-blooded Uptowners and poor folks up the street. But the city was changing. The shuffling of the storm pushed Orleanians out of their comfort zones. That discomfort rallied communities to concretize and promote their needs and values. I knew gatherings like this were in part an advancement of new ideas and people using old social and political power.

I became familiar with the names of the organizers through newspaper articles and television interviews. Local non-profit leaders Karen Cantor; her sister, Martha Hagadorn; and Crescent City Prep Principal Brian Rice had been advertised and sponsored as new hopes for New Orleans' educational system. Katrina made New Orleans ground-zero for market-based reform initiatives that were occurring in Chicago, New York, Philadelphia and L.A. Major foundations could now invest in like-minded organizations that seemed to have unlimited potential for penetration. The national media soon followed.

Karen introduced herself. "So you're the one who writes all those op-eds," she said, eyeing me circumspectly.

"That's me."

"You hail from?"

"Pittsburgh."

"That's funny. You write about needing more local teachers, and you're not local."

Pearly du Bourg's deceased husband, had owned one of the largest beer distilleries in the region, until Pearly sold the business for an amount that catapulted the family to wealth only a few oil families could match. Widowed, she had discretionary time and money, as well as energy that only an unencumbered 63-year-old could have. Pearly gave the maximum contributions allowed to every elected official who could influence her causes. Pearly's entire family all graduated from Catholic schools, but she spent most of her free time on public school reform. Pearly fiercely protected Karen and Martha, who in turn promoted Brian, and they amassed an incredible network of political friends and subsequent enemies in this arena. Nevertheless, friends and foes forewarned me of their reach.

Karen attended Stanford where she majored in political science. She would later receive her graduate degree in engineering from Northwestern University. Martha attended

Yale as an undergrad in the early '90s, participated in Teach for America and later got her M.D. from Harvard, where she met her New Orleans-born husband, who happened to be the son of the president of Allegiance Bank and Trust, the largest regional bank in town.

Karen and Martha worked tirelessly to let other philanthropists in on the window of opportunity that Katrina blew open. They figured the notorious New Orleans public schools would eventually draw superheroes to the Crescent City to manage them. The disreputable story of the valedictorian who could not pass the high school exit examination, dodgy images of "working" security guards donning hair curlers and faux-designer Jackie-O sunglasses, and recordings of the histrionics displayed during official School Board meetings would bring in troops from far and wide to save the schools from despicable old habits. I didn't have a cape, but I'd received an invitation to the "Hall of Justice."

After a brief mixer, Karen called the meeting to order. She presented a chart that displayed the names of failing schools available for charter takeover. She laid out an aggressive strategy to apply for as many charter schools as possible. In the plan, Karen pointed out providers who could manage the schools. Being at the meeting gave me some security that I had some access to information, but I wondered who attended the *meeting before the meeting*. The university had the capacity to manage additional schools, and would be asked. Nevertheless, this gathering provided an opportunity for powerful stakeholders to coordinate and organize.

One school leader who received a major fellowship and grant from the powerful Lockett Foundation said, "We have to move quickly. I heard from a reliable source that the school board has hired a high profile civil rights attorney to take the schools back."

Of the 20 people there, three were Lockett Fellows whom Karen had recruited to New Orleans to "turn around" schools. Lockett promoted market-driven school reform strategies, and takeover was its most aggressive method for change.

Lockett Fellow Madeleine Mitchell joined the conversation. "In order for us to have the greatest impact, we have to open the gates so new human capital can fill these teacher positions."

Karen said, "Let's try to stay focused on getting these schools. I have other plans to present later about how to bring in new teachers."

Brian said, "How are we going to open more schools if we don't have teachers? There's nobody from New Orleans that fits into our school culture."

"We are working on the human capital, but we can't get sidetracked. The state will release its request for charter applications in a few weeks. Martha will give you all technical assistance in filling out the applications."

Martha received millions of dollars to start School Horizons, which provided school leaders with start-up and incubation grants for educational entrepreneurs to develop educational business plans and models while they waited for an opportunity to run a school.

Martha said, "Listen, we have to act now. There are only a few salvageable buildings. We have been working vigorously with the superintendent to pair some of the quick-start facilities with our new charter leaders."

The quick-start program utilized federal disaster relief money to build five brand new schools around the city and remodel several others. These new facilities were built in record time to appease a critical public that the state could in fact move with urgency. The construction companies set the pace for the neighborhood infrastructure. Getting the quick-starts built was one of the rare times when the city pushed the electric company to expedite a new transformer network, which would supply the new schools with power. New Orleans' power infrastructure never served buildings like those the quick-start program created.

Karen interrupted, "Please let's make sure that people are clear about who will take over what schools so we don't have multiple providers applying for the same ones."

Many of the people in the room didn't know me. However, they knew from my writings that I'd favored change, but I was sensitive to community involvement. I surveyed the terrain. Two additional black school leaders generally agreed with the group, showing the fatigue of being the black torch bearers.

The meeting continued as Karen read particular school assignments to the leaders. The educators who moved to New Orleans after the storm did not know the lay of the land well enough to contest assignments. Besides, the pairing was essentially a blessing from one of the most powerful groups in the city to transform a failing school. Who would question and risk not receiving an assignment?

However, the discussion of Armand Lanusse Elementary made me speak. Lanusse Elementary received tremendous attention as it rested in the heart of Treme. Treme was a historic area where free people of color before the Civil War had set up homes and livelihoods sheltering them from the segregationist policies of slavery and Jim Crow; home of St. Augustine Church, where parishioners worshiped before sweating out their starched shirts at second-line parades. It is where Homer Plessy, plaintiff in the landmark Plessy v. Ferguson case, had lived.

Visitors *felt* Treme's difference. Haitian, French and African cultures shine through brass band sweat to scatter into beautiful rainbows of tan. Treme symbolized the Creole stubbornness that resisted highways being built through their neighborhood in the 1960's just as they refused to accept white, bleeding-heart twenty-somethings buying their homes at a frantic pace after Katrina— unsuccessfully.

Treme was more than a neighborhood; it's akin to family. So the idea of taking over a school in Treme from a home Uptown would be as incomprehensible as a Washington, D.C.-based company running hurricane relief projects for New Orleans. However, the charter management organizations in the room looked upon Lanusse Elementary in just that manner.

The group would have formidable opposition. Since my arrival, I regularly heard of the "shadow government" that ran the city. Ironically, I sat in a meeting that could be considered its department of education. I became very familiar with the shadow government of Treme, which fought for decades to maintain an informal independence from the city. Baba Karim, a civil rights activist whose work stems from the segregation battles of the 1970s, would be most offended by not being invited to meetings that involved *his* school. Karim led the charge to change the name of the school from a segregationist one to a free man of color linked to education. His work led to generations of literate public school students who pressed for civil rights in the face of the old Code Noir. Baba Karim held onto his credibility long after most people forgot his work. Like many of his contemporaries, Karim's activism lacked relevancy and technical expertise. In a city that needed rank and file participation, he offered patriarchal representation. And, he represented the people of Treme. He still had the power of voice— literally he became famous for entering forums and shutting down the event with incoherent accusations of institutional oppression and racism. In addition,

Creole landowners from Treme would want complete control as to who would run the school. Neither Uptown nor Treme civic leaders would cede control.

Because of the political powers that still resided in Treme, muckety mucks struck a deal with the state superintendent for it to be the first school in the quick-start program. The community needed a new building as deferred maintenance and neglect ultimately brought death to the original school. Within a year of receiving significant wind damage, the site had to be razed. A new building offered hope and inspiration to a struggling neighborhood where many locals sold property to newcomers seeking to settle in New Orleans. Treme transplants also wanted a new electrical infrastructure in place so they could have the same amenities as they did in places such as San Francisco, D.C., and Chicago.

Karen informed the group of Brian Rice's decision to apply for the failing school. The school would be renamed New Hope Academy. Karen provided ample ammunition for their candidacy. Not only was Armand Lanusse on the bottom of the schools' performance list, but also various neighborhood leaders had sent anonymous letters to the state superintendent soliciting a takeover, and to Brian specifically. The latest unbelievable incident occurred when an Armand Lanusse school security guard handcuffed and shackled a first-grade boy to a chair after an argument with a classmate. These kinds of incidents gave some credence to the need for outside influence.

But, nothing in New Orleans stays secret. As soon as Baba Karim would hear of the meeting and the mentioning of Lanusse Elementary, I knew hell would break loose. Karen knew it too, but she was willing for Brian to feel the flames.

Karen said, "I've learned that Brian is going after Armand

Lanusse Elementary."

The group looked with a blunted astonishment, but no one protested. Karen proceeded to the next school on the alphabetical list. Before she could finish naming the school and expected provider, I interrupted.

"Wouldn't it be wise to get Treme community folks to find a suitable provider?"

Karen asked, "Why? They've had decades to help find an effective school leader."

"You don't think we're setting Brian up for a dangerous political battle, do you?"

"We talked about it. He'll get through the political backlash like UNO did when they took over Johnson."

Unsatisfied I said, "If anything, why don't we get more providers in the city? None of us has proven anything, and we're talking about taking over more schools."

Martha jumped in, "We have several quality providers now. Test scores are up."

I said, "We can't attribute test scores exclusively to what we're doing. Believe it or not, the students and their families may have learned a few things during their evacuations."

One of the black members in the group spoke. "Isaac, we've got to charter as many schools before the board comes alive. Eventually they will."

"The end game can't simply be to charter everything. I thought the goal was to find quality models and effective leaders."

"We have them," Martha repeated.

"I just think it would be prudent to ask the neighborhood what they want."

Karen said emphatically, "They don't want charters. They don't want to change. They would rather fight some stupid ideological battle against charters and let the students suffer."

"Aren't we doing the same?"

Brian inserted himself. "How so?"

"We are essentially saying we are the only ones with the capacity to help the community. I think a lot of us are doing good work, but we were brought in here to prove ourselves, not to ordain ourselves. Why not encourage Treme to find someone on their own? Martha, you have money to do just that. Why not work *with* the community?"

"We fund groups that want to implement best practices."

"Half the people in here never ran a school before arriving in the city. But you took the risk with them."

As young eyes veered my way, I realized I wasn't being a team player. However, I also realized that many of my colleagues had lost the ability to speak when they took grants from the organizers. I knew I needed to back off.

"I just want you all to consider helping the community find a provider."

Karen said, "We'll take that into consideration."

We continued with the school assignments.

Meeting in the Treme

On behalf of Baba Karim, I knew Aramus Strassel requested that I attend a meeting at the African-American Museum, in a historic villa in the heart of the Treme section. Karim earned his stripes as a ferocious activist during the height of the civil rights era. His home and headquarters were in Treme, where he managed a community center. He now was a pillar of a roving civil rights movement that fought against injustices in broad community sectors. Whereas his constituency was less apparent, his voice was as loud and effective as it had been when he was a focused young man. As soon as I received the summons, I knew word circulated back to Karim and the community that the Uptown crowd sought to claim the Armand Lanusse site. Folks also knew that I had access to some inside information, as well as the fact that part of my credibility hinged on providing solutions for the black community. My responses to such calls were integrity checks.

Approximately a dozen residents chatted over finger sandwiches and fruit punch in an upstairs conference room. I was familiar with the brass of Treme, and I knew the allegiances of many in the room. The initial discussions were cautious in anticipation of the tension to come. I could feel the anxiety caused by the inter-neighborhood rumor mill. They heard and believed the Uptown proposal to place one of their providers on the Armand Lanusse site.

I quickly learned how much weight "outsiders" placed on the "shadow government." The shadow government's plans were no more inevitable than those that could be implemented by others. The Treme community needed to put their energy into finding their own solutions instead of reacting to rumors of the Uptown plan.

Even my own employers would demonize people in social circles they perceived they couldn't enter. Even though I was in the room, I was considered a token and couldn't possibly influence decisions. The best I could be was a fly on the wall. The irony was that I realized how fragile ideas from the shadow government were. The Uptown elites needed me as much as the Treme and UNO people did. However, no one trusted my ability to see through the proverbial shadow and into the light.

Eventually, Strassel started the meeting. The group sat as Karim paced angrily along the back wall.

Strassel said, "I've asked y'all to come together to discuss the future of Lanusse. I think we can agree that we need to change providers. As you know, we've heard rumors that someone else is planning for us."

Several pairs of eyes looked toward me.

Strassel continued, "However, we want to make sure that we have a provider that knows what we want as a community."

The recently refurbished Armand Lanusse Elementary was impressive. The state renovated a termite-infested, dilapidated structure where only parents without options would send their child. The new school also proved that renovation can preserve the aesthetics and durable materials of older schools to preserve community landmarks, the sweat equity of the original laborers and New Orleans' architecture. Older residents saw the handiwork and pride that the original tradesmen placed in the building. However, a haphazard educational plan started to dissemble what had been built up.

The new building didn't make children better students. They still fought regularly inside and outside school. Reports of vandalized water fountains, fire alarms and desks accumulated. Lanusse needed a new principal, teachers and staff, as well as a learning philosophy.

Strassel said, "We want what everyone else wants in the community— a quality school where our children get a quality education."

But with a closer look around the room, I determined many present had grandchildren who were school age. Strassel said he was approached by potential suitors for the school but wasn't sure what criteria should be used to evaluate them.

I interjected, "Don't forget about the parents who send their children to Armand Lanusse. We should hear from them."

Karim exploded from the back of the room.

"The people of Treme will decide! I am tired of these *Klansmen* dictating to our children where they should go and who should teach them.

"These are *our* children!" he yelled as he beat his chest. "These people don't care about us. First they say you're going to have options, then they force charters on you. They say you're going to have community input, and then they have Uptowners decide what's best for Downtowners. We're not going to stand for this."

Karim typically reserved histrionics for public meetings, which told me he wanted a message sent to the Uptown crowd.

That's when I started to tune out. In the fight for schools, reformers and resisters made monsters of each other to motivate their bases. If you didn't believe that teetotaling menaces from Uptown lived to oppress black people or that "talentless teachers" from New Orleans, who pay their personal bills during school hours with the checks they collect, then you just weren't passionate enough for the cause. I looked onto my notepad hoping someone would crack the glacier Karim had formed.

Strassel continued where he left off.

"Dr. Boyd, can you help us locate a provider?"

"Absolutely. I think we can start by potentially teaching you how to fill out a charter application. Then you can see what it entails."

As I started to explain the application process and what dispositions one should look for in a provider, Karim interrupted.

"I would rather not have a school if we don't run it. What good is a school if our people aren't running it? We can't always be the ones receiving knowledge from some white person who has been here five minutes."

I replied, "I agree. We need *quality* homegrown talent to take charge of our schools. But we can't succeed in this charter vs. non-charter, black vs. white environment, either."

Irritated by my comment, Karim said, "I don't have a problem with charter schools. I have a problem with someone telling us how to run our schools."

My face fell as I considered how many families were underserved by public education in the past. New Orleans needed help in getting the system stabilized. The city needed new teachers, innovation and creativity. To expect different outcomes using the same people and model seemed illogical. However, I understood that the community would have to sustain the innovations that came with reform.

Strassel looked at me and asked, "How do we choose the next group to run the school?"

"The same way Uptown would— by asking. We know who knows how to run a successful school. We also know who has the capacity to turn around a failing school. The problem is that quality providers are in short supply. You have to seek them out."

"How?"

"I think it would be helpful for you and a few teachers that you trust to read the charter application and see what's expected. There are tons of details, but I also help evaluate applications so I can help decipher them for you."

A woman at the table said, "I've seen the application. I don't know if we can pull it off in time for the next school year."

I said, "It's definitely like eating an elephant. You take one bite at a time."

"The insurances, budgetary details, curriculum guidelines; I was a teacher and I don't think I could respond to many of the questions in the application."

I said, "Every day someone from outside New Orleans is taking the time. It can be done."

Strassel asked, "How long is the application?"

"A charter proposal can range from 250 to 400 pages."

My response discouraged Strassel. I tried to dislodge the disappointment.

I said, "If everyone at this table takes a small part of the application we can get it done more efficiently.

Karim bellowed, "They're going to give schools to the applicants they want. We can't let them in here."

I thought to myself, too many pronouns and generalizations. Continuously saying "no" wouldn't get a good provider nor would it change the conditions that children labored under today.

I said, "This could be an opportunity for our historically black colleges and universities to re-enter the school reform conversation." Dillard, Xavier and Southern universities produced most of the great teachers and educational leaders in the city from Reconstruction to the 1980s. While hundreds of former New Orleans School Board teachers approached retirement or were forced into early retirement, they had seen and implemented multiple reforms in the past. Unfortunately, their children, the city's future generations of teachers, saw public school conditions worsen as their professional options increased. The children of the great teaching generations chose professions other than education. Consequently, the past twenty years did not offer students the bright, energetic teachers their parents had.

To make matters worse, the vested public school teachers sent their children to parochial and private schools— depriving the system of socioeconomic diversity. As the educational needs of impoverished communities intensified, the teacher talent pool shrank and belief in public schools waned.

I said, "Getting quality teachers who happen to be black won't be easy. We can't afford not to find people who have the energy and smarts to work in very challenging conditions. Y'all know what it's like when no one in the family has a college degree. We need people to struggle with our children as they are forced to learn. You simply can't limit the pool to black people. The reality is we will need a strong, diverse labor pool."

A brave voice spoke from the table.

"I agree. This isn't a fight for black personnel. This is a fight for good schools and community involvement."

I followed up immediately.

"You're exactly right. You need to make sure the community

surrounding the school has some, not all, influence as to what large organizations come into its space. Look, a bad school environment can be as dangerous to the neighborhood as a manufacturing plant that doesn't care about environmental issues."

Refocusing the conversation, Strassel asked, "Who can help?"

I replied, "Approach Xavier and Dillard about sponsoring your application. Their faculty can write it, recruit its best teacher candidates and hire some of its best alums. You can sit on the board and provide insight from a neighborhood perspective."

Another participant at the table said, "I don't think they will do it. They've been trying to eliminate their educational programs since the storm."

Karim still chimed in from the rear, "You think you're going to wait for black colleges to get our children civil rights? We have to march up in those meetings and tell these white folks, hell no!"

I said calmly, "Some of our black colleges need a nudge to get back into the laboratory school game. Dillard and Xavier have too much experience with running schools not to. Getting an application approved is as much about fiscal capacity as it is about managerial competence. The colleges are well suited."

The group looked satisfied with the initial strategy. However, Karim was stubborn.

He said, "We have teachers. We have a system. You're going to let these white people and sell-outs take our schools away from us? Over my dead body!"

After his outburst, I agreed to arrange a meeting between university leaders and the Treme group. I bid the group adieu.

Let the Politics Begin

As students entered the class for the first day of politicking, the class newspaper had already projected a winner. Students called out both real and political "stage" names.

"Loren, Lee Ferguson, Loren, Lee," came from all directions. Instead of answering the calls, Loren scanned the faux-newspaper. The headline Mr. Simon, Charles van Collins, distributed to the raucous group of politicians, interest groups, and citizens read, "Are there any questions? Eight long years for Green." The article opened with, "Green's insurmountable lead is as large as the candidate's adoring public… Lee Ferguson and the Democratic Party should consider conceding the election to save time, money, and save face." With anger and disbelief, Loren looked at his sheet of characters for help. The first name to leap from the page was Carl Prentice, who played his press secretary, Ronald Weathers.

Loren searched the room for Carl. As everyone networked, he spotted Carl among a group who wore press badges around their necks. Loren yelled his name.

"Carl… Carl… over here."

A few students in Carl's group looked toward Loren briefly and then resumed their duties. Carl didn't acknowledge Loren.

Loren knew Carl had heard him.

Loren walked toward him, then looked Carl directly in the eyes and said, "You heard me."

Carl said sourly, "My name is Ronald Weathers, press secretary. Have you read the headlines?"

"Your name is Carl, and I want to talk about the headlines." They moved away from the group.

"My name is *Ronald Weathers* and I think we need to resolve this issue. If you want to be president, you play the game."

Loren was irritated.

"Ronald Weathers, *press secretary*, tell me what's going on?"

Carl said, "Because you were late for school *again*, you missed an important event. The press asked for comments from both candidates. Your opponent Tracy Green took advantage of the situation. She made comments about you showing up late for school and how you hang out with shady people. Ms. Green said, 'I hope my opponent realizes the seriousness of this election.' I told the media that you had a doctor's appointment and would be arriving late today."

"Katura said that?"

"Ms. Green said those exact words."

Loren said, "I thought mudslinging was a bad thing."

"I think you should make a comment about her tactics and how she is straying from the political issues."

"You're my press secretary. Help me write something!"

"What?

"Something about mudslinging and straying from facts."

Carl asked, "What facts are Ms. Green straying from?"

Carl was definitely playing the game. He asked, "What exactly *is* your platform? What issues are you promoting? If you want to make a statement about getting back to the issues, then have some."

Loren sighed. "You're right."

"Well, you don't have much time. The election is in a week. If you don't have a platform, Green will eat you for lunch. She's talking about creating a 'Family Day' at Johnson. She's also pushing for a gospel choir trip to New York City."

"When did she do all this?"

"While you were *late*," Carl said sarcastically.

"Don't forget that I still call myself Loren, and I never let you diss me in the past. Don't think I am going to let you do it now."

"Mr. Ferguson, I suggest we argue less over names, more over platforms."

"All right, create a press release stating that I will unveil my peer-mentoring program tomorrow morning."

"What peer-mentoring program?"

"The one that I'm going to announce tomorrow. Do your job and get me some time on the microphone and a little print in the paper. Also, get me some flyers on the wall."

"Now we're moving, Lee Ferguson, democratic presidential candidate."

"I told you, call me Loren."

Flyers with Katura's "Tracy Green" face were posted around the room. After examining the list of presidential characters, Loren finally found his campaign manager, "Marcus Pearson," played by his good friend Clarence.

"How can I help you Mr. Ferguson?"

"Look, I'm all for playing the game, but call me Loren. Anyway Clarence, I need you to set up a meeting with the junior class president and the head guidance counselor."

Clarence asked, "What's going on?"

"Listen closely. Carl is going to make an announcement

about the new peer-mentoring program I'm creating. I need the junior class president and guidance counselors to say this sort of program is allowed."

"Peer mentoring? What's that?"

Loren said, "Peer mentoring— what does it sound like?"

Clarence looked at Loren blankly.

"I want to set up a program where older students help freshmen with their studies. Get a pass from Mr. Simon, Charles van Collins, or whatever his name is, and get down to the counselors' office to get me a pass for the sixth period."

"They won't give me a pass for you."

"Yes, they will. Mr. Simon gets everybody passes because of this election."

"What else do you want me to do, Lee Ferguson?"

"Ask who the junior class president is and set up a lunch meeting, then get an appointment with the guidance counselor for sixth period."

Loren grabbed Clarence's shoulder and asked, "Where did *Ms. Green* get all those flyers."

"You know Katura's father is pastor for the church Mr. Simon goes to. She can use the church or school's copying machines. Katura also goes to church with Drea, who plays the pollster person. That's why she's pushing the gospel choir thing. The gospel choir has been trying to get a trip to New York. If you didn't notice, half of the girls in the class are *in* gospel choir, and they go to Katura's, I mean *Ms. Green's* father's church. You know she's getting their votes. When you put two and two together, it equals advantage."

"Mr. Simon can't allow that," Loren said angrily.

"Mr. Simon isn't allowing it, Charles van Collins is. It's confusing."

"How am I going to make copies?"

Clarence laughed and said, "Start going to church. Ferguson, you basically have four groups to suck up to. You have the church girls. You can't get their votes. You can get the thugs. I can make them vote for you. The two wild cards are the nerds and the nobodies— you can get them. If we didn't pick on those nerds, we could get their votes. But I noticed that you have a couple of friends in that clique. I don't know why you hang with nerd James, but he can help."

Loren said, "It's not like I hang with him every day."

"Whatever, Lee Ferguson. You know you're two peas in a pod. I don't choose your friends. Tell James to pump you up. You can win this election with some good press."

"I'm still working on getting flyers and handing out some press releases."

Clarence went for the pass, and Loren checked the character sheet for more help. Suddenly he was bumped in the back.

"Excuse me, Mr. Ferguson."

Loren recognized Katura's voice. "What a pleasant surprise. Ms. Green. How are you doing?"

"According to the polls, quite well."

"That's not hard when you're singing 'Wade in the Water' with the pollster every Sunday."

As Katura backed toward the other side of the room, she said with a broad smile, "You know Mr. Ferguson, the Bible tells us to love our neighbors and do good to our enemies."

"Practice what you preach, Ms. Green." Loren's eyes returned to the character sheet. Instead of looking at his staff, Loren began to peruse Tracy Green's. He saw that Martin Mouton, A.K.A. Charlie Astin, was the PR/marketing director for the Green campaign, and also attended Katura's church. Loren checked to see what Martin was doing in class and found him on a ladder taping up flyers. Martin was one of the gen. ed. kids and owed Loren a favor he needed to call in.

Between meetings and interviews, Loren frantically thought about the peer-mentoring program that could pull votes. He pondered the advantage Katura had. The Green campaign controlled the media, and had non-school resources and a large constituency.

Before class ended, Clarence returned with meeting times from the counselor and with the junior class president. Clarence had a look of accomplishment.

"Good, news Mr. President. Sean Adu will meet you during lunch and Ms. Richardson will meet you in her office at the start of the sixth period."

"Give me the pass."

Loren snatched it from Clarence and said, "My man— you really hooked me up."

Clarence was curious.

"Whose class are you going to cut?"

"Who do you think?"

After a brief pause, they laughed in unison. "McClain."

At that point, the bell rang for the second period. Loren told Clarence to have Carl meet them at the usual lunch spot. In the meantime, Loren had to sell program ideas to various constituencies and find a way to get print space. Clarence and Loren parted with a pound, a ghetto handshake, and a plan.

* * *

Lunchtime in the cafeteria was an intense negotiation session. The ninth-grade section of the cafeteria buzzed with political deal making. The rest of school were curious spectators. Loren met his press secretary and campaign manager in the hall and walked shoulder to shoulder into the cafeteria. Loren felt eyes on them as they strode through the door. The Green party reserved a table in the corner closest to the entrance. Her team of several young women gave an impression of an organized front. Katura's station forced everyone to pass her table to get lunch. She handed out flyers about her gospel choir initiative.

Green's was not the only group that added to the ambiance. The outsiders' speculation contributed to the lively atmosphere. Everyone wanted to know campaign details and dirt. The entire school felt the excitement of a good contest. But James envied their participation. Many honors students who could not take regular civics with Mr. Simon felt that Simon's election should have occurred on the other side of the school.

James said, "The school should select candidates from general education and honors tracks."

James said if the entire class could vote, then why couldn't they nominate candidates? The fact was Mr. Simon was the only teacher who wanted to perform such an exercise, which prohibited an inclusive election. No other teacher wanted to distract students from studying for the upcoming state exam. Despite his legitimate protest, Simon's students considered James' demands as invasive calls for inclusion. He talked about the election as if the possibility existed that he could be selected to run. However, many sympathized with James because the election was such fun, and the need for more participants was apparent. A case in point was that each of the candidates had seven staff members. Most did satisfactory work. But they could have used additional support.

Because James could not officially participate, he lived

vicariously through Loren's campaign. James was visibly excited at hearing the news. After a loud greeting in the hall, James immediately gave Loren advice. His honors courses gave him an edge, he said, and he was more than willing to assist the candidate. He sought involvement one way or another. Loren excused himself for his cafeteria meeting, but James followed.

On the way, Loren considered feeding James' ego by making him a friend of the party. James didn't need to know that Loren didn't want his advice. But the Ferguson camp needed help getting votes and with other mundane jobs.

As the Ferguson team approached the center of the cafeteria, James had worked his way across their path. Loren's campaign manager, Clarence, let loose an aggrieved sigh. Carl laughed at Clarence's reaction.

Clarence fumed said, "If it isn't the most annoying person on earth. I hear your mother drops you off at school two hours early just to get you out the house."

James said, "Does your mother even know you're *in* school?"

Loren grabbed Clarence's forearm to indicate that he should relax.

Loren said, "James, can you find us a table to do work? I have a big assignment for you." Clarence knew why Loren needed James and he regretted recommending James as an entrée to the honors student population.

James said, "I'm on it."

Loren said, "Look for us in about fifteen minutes. We have a meeting on the 11th grade side."

"Anything I can do?"

"Just get us a table. We'll be back." Loren pushed James away and Carl, Clarence, and he headed across the hall to the old gym, which was overflow cafeteria seating. Eleventh and 12th-graders ate there.

As they approached the entrance, the assistant principal called down the hall, "Where do you think you're going?"

Clarence said, "We have a meeting with the junior class president. It's for the election."

Loren reached in his pocket, pulled up a yellow sheet of paper and said, "Here's our pass."

The assistant principal then said, "OK, make it quick. I'll be looking for y'all."

Before the group entered the upperclass haven, they adjusted their clothes and attitudes. They nodded in readiness, then opened the door. When they entered the gym, Loren's crew immediately noticed one significant difference between the lower and upper sides— the girls. For about ten seconds, they stood in awe of the pretty faces and more adult bodies that turned momentarily to glance at them. The girls' eyes returned to their meals and conversations when they recognized Loren was an underclassman. However, the boys' eyes remain glued on them. Only juniors and seniors were allowed there. The normally cool Clarence was speechless. Sean Abu greeted them at the door.

"What's up?"

The awestruck trio stood silent at his greeting.

Knowing the girls stunned them, Sean repeated, "Yeah, the ladies are fine, huh? So what's the story?"

Loren said, "Nothing much. I am Lee Ferguson … I mean Loren, and this is Clarence and Carl also known as Mr. Marcus Pearson and Mr. Ron Weathers."

Sean started laughing and said, "You guys have Mr. Simon, don't you?"

They said in chorus, "Yes."

Feeling more comfortable, Loren said, "So you know what

we're trying to do?"

Sean said, "Not really. When Clarence came to me, I knew about the election thing, but I wasn't sure what you wanted. I thought 9th-graders were the only voters."

"They are, but I have an idea that helps me and the school."

With a slight chuckle, Sean said, "Yes, Mr. Ferguson?"

"I want to start a peer-mentoring program for freshmen. The 12th-graders would mentor 9th-graders."

"I'm the *junior* class president."

"But you know all the girls and guys admire you. You'll be senior president next year."

Sean was impressed by Loren's forward thinking. He had no idea that Loren's idea was off the cuff.

He asked, "What do you want?"

"An endorsement. I want to announce this program tomorrow in a press conference and our newspaper, and I want your name behind it."

"What else?"

"I want the honors society to be mentors for the program."

Clarence didn't understand Loren's tack.

Loren said, "The 9th-grade honors students will choose me if they see themselves being mentored by other honors students, and if they see themselves as mentors one day."

Sean said, "You've done your homework, son. I guess you know I'm a junior honors society officer, and I think this is a good school service project for us."

"Can you talk to your members by tonight? I want to put your name on our flyers and include it in my platform as well."

"I got you."

"Thanks." Loren extended his hand to seal the deal. "I'll talk to you later."

"All right Mr. Ferguson."

Loren, Clarence and Carl took a final glance at their future lunchroom and headed out.

Back in the lower class cafeteria, the room still buzzed, and the Green party handed Loren a flyer. The headline read, "Tracy Green— We're takin' it to the next level."

He told the volunteer, "You should change it to 'Tracy Green— A trip to New York.' Katura smiled at Loren as he passed by.

"Mr. Ferguson! Mr. Ferguson! I have a table." James pulled Loren towards a table as Clarence groaned and Carl laughed.

James said, "You took a bit longer than expected, so I took the liberty of getting your lunches."

Clarence said, "You're the biggest suck-up in the world."

But Loren interrupted, "Good work, James. There isn't much time to eat so let's get busy."

They sat down and Clarence burned in frustration before he reluctantly began eating.

"So we have a program. We still don't have flyers," Carl said.

"What program?" James asked.

But Loren answered Carl.

"You have a computer class this afternoon. You can make flyers."

Carl said, "Right. I can put something together."

"Keep it simple. The most important part of the flyer should be my name and the peer-mentoring program. Then, just talk about how incoming 9th-grade students will be paired with seniors. I need you to make the flyer general so that later I can include guidance office info. I also need you to get paper from the class and finished flyers to Clarence."

James said, "What's the guidance office doing?"

Loren ignored him to save time.

Carl asked, "What about copies? How are we going to run copies?"

"Get me the original and Clarence the paper by sixth period. You can find me in the counselors' office. We'll get you copies."

Loren looked at Clarence and said, "We have to call in a favor."

The two looked at each and said simultaneously, "Martin!"

"Martin who owes his life to us."

"Yep."

"Damn, you're good," Clarence laughed.

Loren laughed too as James asked, "Who's Martin?"

Clarence said, "Martin is minding his business like you should be." His warning stopped James, but Loren smoothed the confrontation.

"James, you have to tell folks that peer mentoring will pair senior honors society members with new students. Tell them this gives honors students an opportunity to work with older honors students. You have to get me their votes. I will keep you posted on other things tomorrow. You're an important member of this team, and I need you to come through."

"You've got those votes."

"Clarence, meet me after school by the old white guy. We have an appointment with— Martin." The bell sounded and the students parted.

Typically at the end of school, Loren and his friends met at the large, white-marble bust of former President Lyndon B. Johnson, which faced the west exit doors. School leaders salvaged it from the rubble of the destroyed Johnson site. Although it served as a common area and meeting place, few people introduced themselves to Lyndon B. People walked passed Johnson as if he was a persistent admirer you purposely try to avoid. However,

Loren was different.

In order to get to Mr. McClain's sixth period English course, Loren had to pass Katura's Algebra class and the bust. Katura often took her time to leave class just so she could watch Loren examine Johnson's head. She often caught Loren reading the inscriptions on the bust's platform: "The test before us as a people is not whether our commitments match our will and our courage; but whether we have the will and courage to match our commitments."

* * *

After Loren received the confirmation and endorsement from the guidance office, he made small talk with Principal Sarnacola so he could skip Mr. McClain's class. The guidance office and principal appreciated that his platform would not just benefit freshmen. They assured Loren that if elected they would provide the resources and administrative support for his peer mentoring. Carl gave Loren the flyer and paper for Clarence. All Loren needed was a copy machine. He tried to get copies from the main office, but the secretaries copied textbooks all afternoon.

Before classes ended for the day, Loren paced on the school's west exit gallery. He watched Clarence run toward him. He'd skipped last period, too. Loren jumped down the stairs. Clarence walked back toward school to meet Loren.

Clarence said sarcastically, "You'd better get away before someone catches you. I got a pass to skip class. Did you?" Clarence opened his backpack and showed four reams of paper.

"Now all we need is copies."

"What exit does Martin come from?"

As the final bell sounded, Loren said, "He should be out this door in a few minutes. Martin always tries to get out early. His parents pick him up from the church down the street. Don't worry, we'll get him."

After waiting about ten minutes, Martin emerged from the crowd. He carried a large knapsack of flyers and scurried down the steps. Clarence and Loren carefully watched him. Martin eventually made his way down the street. Martin stopped once or twice to post flyers. Once he cleared a few blocks, Loren and Clarence caught up with him.

"Martin, wait a second."

Clarence barely held in his laughter as they approached Martin.

"Where are you headed?" Loren asked after a light jog. Martin walked as they talked.

"You're supposed to call me Charlie Astin. Did you forget my name, Mr. Ferguson?"

"No, I didn't forget your name, but we'll stick with the real ones."

Martin said, "I respect that. So what's up?"

Loren replied, "Let me ask you again. Where you headed?"

"I'm going to church. Why?"

Loren said, "Katura's flyers are copied there."

"What are you talking about?" Martin chuckled. "You mean Ms. Green. You know that is privileged information."

Clarence snorted, "You don't have privileged information. *We* have privileged information."

Martin was tight-lipped. "This is not part of the game, Loren."

Loren said, "I hope you're taking me seriously. All we want to know is if you can make us some copies at the church."

"I don't know what you're talking about."

Loren pulled out the flyer that Carl made, and Clarence

pulled out the paper.

"I am asking you to do me a favor and make copies for me."

"I can't."

"Why not?" Clarence asked.

"Because I'm working for your opponent."

Loren said, "I know who's doing what for whom. I am asking for a favor from someone who owes us one."

Loren paused for a moment, looked up in the sky, and used a voice reminiscent of an old English storyteller with a ghetto twist.

"Ahh, it was a hot summer's evening not so long ago. The boys and I were frolicking in the streets when someone decided we should play some football."

Clarence laughed at the accent.

Loren continued, "We were not too far from your house when I realized we were short one player. So I ran to your house to see if you wanted to join in. I thought including you was a good idea since you've got *good hands*. Don't you think that was decent of me, Clarence?"

"You should be considered a philanthropist."

"There was only one problem. We saw your parents' car, and we all know they don't like you playing street football.

"So out of the kindness of our hearts we went around the side of your house to knock on your window and get you from your room.

"Before my hand could knock on your window, I closed my eyes several times to make sure I wasn't seeing naked men and women on your television. I had to ask my colleague to look for himself."

"Your eyes saw as perfectly as mine. There were naked body parts all over the screen," Clarence said.

"The distraction was so great that I almost didn't notice that your pants were around your ankles."

Clarence told Loren, "You were very distracted. I had to point out that Martin's pants were around his ankles."

"Then I became concerned about your health, Martin."

Martin fumed.

"If your parents knew what you were doing, they would certainly try to exorcise the demons from your body. So I had to knock on the window to get your attention. I will never forget the promise you made to Clarence and me. You said if we didn't tell, you would do anything for us."

"'Anything! Anything! Anything!' were his exact words," Clarence said.

Dropping the accent, Loren said, "I want copies made and delivered to my house before seven tonight. Here is the flyer and the paper."

Loren handed everything to Martin as he stood stupefied.

"Thank you, *Martin*. A pleasure doing business with you."

Loyalty

Katura should have been nervous at Loren's door. Ms. Rena didn't like young ladies on her doorstep after sunset. Not only was it 10 p.m., but it was also a school night. Katura argued her parents into allowing the visit. Knowing the importance of the election, she appealed to their sympathies. Uncharacteristically, Katura lied and told them Ms. Rena agreed to a brief visit. She asked to drop some flyers off that Loren needed for the election. Katura showed her parents the flyer Martin made for Loren at the church, and asked if she could review some details with him before tomorrow morning. Katura's parents waited until Ms. Rena's door opened. They'd be back in thirty minutes. That gave her time to handle Loren.

Loren's mom found Katura at her door with no parents in tow, but watched their car pull away.

"What brings you here so late, and why are your parents leaving?"

"I need to talk to Loren about the election."

Ms Rena leaned in and hugged the girl.

"Congratulations, baby. Loren told me you two are running against each other. Sounds exciting, but you know you have to do schoolwork. I can't have young girls visiting here this late."

"I would never disrespect your home, Ms. Rena, but Loren needs these flyers, and we need to review our election assignments. We were so busy we didn't finish our work. I promise I'll be no more than a half hour." Rena eyed her skeptically.

Katura kept on. "I tried calling, but someone was on the phone."

After a brief pause, Rena said, "I'll get Loren and you two can work in the living room while I clean the kitchen."

"Thank you, Ms. Rena."

Rena called up the stairs.

"Son, you have company."

She told Katura to have a seat in the living room. Katura knew Ms. Rena would give Loren a short talk about having girls over late. Ms. Rena didn't care if he didn't invite her. Katura was also sure he would suffer an extended version later.

Ms. Rena left. Then Katura heard Loren's halting walk down the steps. Loren sat across from Katura.

Looking askance at her, he said, "Well?"

"I just wanted to deliver your flyers." She held up what Martin printed. Loren mustered the courage to look at her. Katura kept talking nonchalantly.

"What kind of game do you think you're playing?"

"The same one you are," Loren snapped.

She only had a few minutes, so she had to be civil. She thought of burning Loren's flyers, or stuffing some down his throat. Instead she channeled her rage.

"You're using outside help to win this election," Loren said.

"What's wrong with using the resources I have?"

"What happens if I don't have those resources, Katura?"

"You *steal* them! Real ethical."

"You didn't play fair, so why should I?"

"Let's get one thing straight. I didn't do anything wrong. We're supposed to use resources we have to accomplish our goals. Are you trying to blame me for having access to a copying machine?"

"We should have access to the same resources. Then we'll see who uses the same materials best."

"Same materials the best? Who's been tutoring you the past year?"

Rena heard raised voices.

"Is everything OK?"

"Yes, Ma. We're arguing a point," Loren said.

Adjusting her voice Katura said, "We both know there's nothing equal in elections. Everyone has different resources. You need to exploit yours."

"What are you saying Katura? Flyers are going to fall from the sky at my door?"

"Loren, maybe you should get people on your staff who can think instead of imitate. You're so busy doing what I am that you aren't being creative."

"Everyone knows you need flyers to win the election."

"You need publicity, not flyers. Candidates use different types of publicity to get votes."

"Get real, Katura. I need flyers to get the word out."

"So your solution was to bully my staff member to get what you wanted." Katura lowered her voice to stifle her anger. "Let me tell you something. If you threaten any of my staff again, I'll tell Mr. Simon."

Loren looked at the ceiling for a moment.

After thinking over her threat, Katura said, "I think I am going to tell Mr. Simon anyway."

"You can't do that."

"Why not?"

"Because we're friends."

"If we were friends, you could've asked me."

"You weren't going to let me use the church machine."

"Why wouldn't I? I don't let this election get in the way of friendship."

Loren was floored.

"First you bully my staff member. Then you go behind my back. I thought you were better than that. The only idea you're loyal to is yourself."

"I did what I thought I had to do to get flyers."

"So it's like that? You never even thought I would help."

"It's easy for you to say this when you have everything. I'm taking this election seriously."

Loren used an intellectual tack.

"Make sure you utilize all the actors, resources, and strategies afforded to you," is what Mr. Simon said. Listen, Katura. I don't know anybody, and I don't have anything. Yeah, you're my friend, but we're opponents in this race. I needed flyers, and did what I had to do. If you'd wanted me to have flyers, you could've offered to print them from the start."

"I brought these flyers over here to give to you. I'm here to remind you, you could have asked. Some rules you don't break."

Katura's parents knocked on the door. She got up and set the copies on the table. Rena let her out. She told Katura good night and said hello to her folks. Katura gave Rena a hug and a thank you.

Rena held her for the slightest moment and said, "No. Thank you."

Ms. Rena gave Katura a wink, and the girl returned it with a smile.

Master Plan

Loren was embarrassed, then depressed. When he came up with his extortion plan, getting caught hadn't entered his mind. Even though he felt justified, Katura made him squirm. He felt more shame from disappointing Katura than bullying Martin. Katura's tirade blindsided him. Childhood ethics generally boiled down to do's and don'ts, wrongs and "I'm going to beat your butt." Katura veered from that script. As soon as she chastised him, she left, leaving him to reflect. Loren thought he'd betrayed a friend, election notwithstanding.

He also considered the fairness of elections when candidates had different financial resources. Mr. Simon could have allowed equal finances or provided more rigid guidelines. But it seemed that access to personal resources made it difficult for the poorer candidate. The only resources Loren had were friends, and Katura wasn't going to finance his campaign. The idea that Katura could buy her friends' votes through a trip to New York incensed him. The more Loren thought about the situation, the angrier he became.

Anger and competition can fuel ingenuity. However, the urgency of the situation mitigated his anger. Loren needed to respond quickly, or he would lose the election. He paced the spot where Katura left him as if he were trying to calm himself. Loren took a deep breath and sat on the stairs. One thing was clear; he needed a way to deploy his platform. Voters didn't have a sense of what or how he could improve the school or their personal situations. Katura's posters all over school highlighted his weakness as an organizer and his economic status.

Loren didn't want to use the flyers that Katura brought. He was too proud and ashamed to consider them. The next few hours were critical. He couldn't afford to waste another day. He needed another brain to help him. Katura was unavailable, so he chose the next best option, Clarence.

Loren ran into the kitchen to ask his mom if Clarence could spend the night to work on his election. Sensing his need, she agreed. Loren called, telling him about Katura's visit, and Clarence agreed they needed to brainstorm.

It was nearly eleven when Clarence arrived. Ms. Rena went to bed after letting him in.

"Wait till I get a hold of that snitch! That dude is done!"

Loren whispered, "Shhh! My mom is trying to sleep, and besides, Katura just got even."

Clarence lowered his voice, "I'm still going to get him."

Loren moved to the kitchen, sat on the bottom step and said, "We have to think of something now."

Clarence paced feverishly.

"We have to win this election, Loren."

"When did you get so interested in schoolwork?"

"I'm not really. I just want to win."

"Well, in order to win, we need to present our campaign strategy."

"We got all this stuff to do and I have a football game tomorrow," Clarence said.

"Football game?"

Clarence said, "How can you forget about Prep versus Johnson?"

As Clarence spoke, Loren placed his head in his lap and listened. His wheels started turning. Finally, he stated enthusiastically, "That's it. We've got football— the biggest draw in town. We can present our campaign at the game!"

"Yeah!"

A few good ideas bubbled up. Loren and Clarence both paced. By 11:30, Clarence devised a master plan.

"Seriously, why does Mr. McClain feel he can harass us? Why do 12th-graders think they can take our basketballs? Why does Prep think they can piss on us and walk away with a victory?"

The J.V. football team had lost the last two games with Prep, and the team lost face with the student body.

Loren faced Clarence knowing the answer, "Respect."

"Respect."

"How can we use *respect* to spread our platform?"

Clarence said, "We need a catchy slogan. Something simple like 'Say no to drugs.'" They laughed and between chuckles Loren conjured up one.

"What about, 'We run for respect'?"

A smile spread over Clarence's face, then added to the idea.

"Try this on for size. We're supposed to wear shirts and ties for game day. Why don't I get the team to open doors for the ladies throughout the day as we pass out our flyers?— Respect."

"Will the team go for that?"

Clarence said, "They will if I ask them to."

Katura's words about bullying were still fresh in Loren's head, so he said, "I don't know."

"Look, we can't be scared. It's a good idea. We have to run

with it."

Loren shook off his fears. "We can lay out our slogan on the other side of our flyer, even though it has nothing to do with mentoring."

Clarence said, "'Run with respect' is the hook. We'll hit them with our agenda when we lure those fish in. The ladies will love it."

"We'll pump up the fans by promoting the game *and* the election."

Loren began to think out the logistics and was sobered by the work ahead.

"We still need to make flyers and contact the team."

"My little brother can do a flyer. I will tell him to spell respect, R.E.S.P.E.X.T."

Loren didn't get it. "With an *X*?"

"Every time the team does something on the field, the players on the sideline will cross their forearms and make an *X*. The team and fans will eat it up."

"But how about the flyers?"

"Man, you can charm one of those secretaries. You want to win? Get to school early and show those pearly whites."

"Why don't you ask?"

"Because my teeth are too crooked."

Loren looked nervous.

Clarence got in his face.

"You want to win?

Then Clarence stepped back and smiled.

But Loren looked at his watch. "How are we going to get the team involved at this hour?"

Clarence said, "I'll call them up, text them, and get on MySpace. If I get a parent, I'll say it's football-related. Besides, it's not like there's a lot of players to call. We only need the top ones. We'll be done by 12:15."

"Let's move."

Everything went smoothly. Team members showed up early in blazers and ties to open doors for students and faculty throughout the day. They handed out the new flyers. Students, faculty, and staff appreciated the gentlemanly gestures. Clarence, Carl, and Loren posted flyers around the school and football field. Students buzzed about the slogan and mentoring program. Things could not have gone better. The tide shifted, and Loren and Clarence found themselves driving the election. All Loren needed was a good showing at the football game.

After the first play of the game, an exciting catch in the school's favor ushered in X signs. The crowd caught the spirit. Before the end of the first half, the X marked the spot all over the stands and the team was ahead fourteen points. They started a new craze and a new phase. Loren had the election in the bag.

Life Coach

Loren had been running after school every day for the last few months. Slowly his weak leg grew stronger. His one- to two-mile jogs became five-mile runs. With every stride, Loren gained confidence and muscle. He typically ran a loop through the neighborhood back to school in order to shower. It wasn't until I saw Loren pass football and basketball players on training runs did I imagine the possibility of starting a running program. I inherited the basketball and football teams because that was what New Orleans' high schools did. I forgot I had broader choices. Sure, parents reminded me how important football and basketball were to the community. And the games brought revenue schools could put back into their athletic programs. But New Orleans needed another football or basketball star as much as another rapper.

Loren could be the new wave of athleticism. So I located one of the best cross-country and track coaches in the city, Joseph Drayton, better known as Coach D. St. Benedict's Academy laid off Drayton after the storm. Track and field was the only sport of note at St. Benedict's. Even though Drayton won multiple Catholic League titles, his accomplishments couldn't salvage his job on a tight post-storm budget. At Johnson, Coach D. taught history and P.E. in the upper grades, so he didn't know Loren. I planned an introduction.

Coach D.'s reputation preceded him. His one affectation was an impeccable wardrobe, which became the talk of the school. I wondered why so many black youths deferred to this urbane, middle-aged Italian American who never appeared to wear the same outfits twice. Ball players didn't approach their coaches in the same manner. Students could talk to coaches, but a level of tension always lingered.

We waited for Loren in the breezeway to the locker room. When he approached Coach D. and me, he looked surprised.

Before he could say a word, Coach asked, "Loren?"

Loren's voice quivered as he said, "Yes sir," revealing he was nervous.

"Pleasure meeting you. I'm Coach Drayton. I'm the new track and field and cross-country coach."

"I see you around school," Loren said more calmly.

"It's good to meet a young man who runs on his own. I used to run to school when I was your age. A coach inspired me." Drayton paused at the long-ago memory.

"How many miles did you just run?"

"Five," Loren said, waiting for the coach's verdict on this distance.

"Really? Dr. Boyd told me you've been running after school every day for the last two months. People don't run that far unless they love it. You seem to. What made you start?"

"My mother and I made a deal."

"Well, whatever the deal was, it looks like it's turned out a win-win," Coach D. laughed. Loren laughed, too, and said, "She knew what she was doing."

"What grade are you in son?"

"Ninth."

"Did you ever do track or cross country?"

"No."

"I like motivated athletes. Do you play other sports, Loren?"

"No. I just run. And I'm getting better," Loren said proudly.

"My running program requires a big commitment. If you're not studying, you should be running."

A smile exploded across Loren's face. He'd waited a lifetime to be part of a team, and I could feel his happiness. Basketball seemed like one, big painful stereotype. Although I appreciated the sports, I despised my football coaches' embracing the "hood gladiator" trope. No matter how low their talent levels, inner-city ball teams fancied themselves as farm leagues to college and professional leagues. Moreover, the coaches taught players to fear them. This shackled students' creative spirits on field and academic spirits off. Coaches forced teamwork with iron fists. I always said, if I had to start a school fresh, I wouldn't offer ball teams.

After exchanging a few more pleasantries, Coach D. opened the door and asked us to walk to his office. He asked Loren how he trained. Then Coach D. gave Loren a list of additional exercises to perform after Monday, Wednesday, and Friday runs. Coach told Loren if he continued this new program, he would be ready to run with the varsity cross-country team by his sophomore year. Loren had a new dream to chase.

Stolen Moments

The evening of the 9th-grade formal was to be the best of Katura's life. Her Aunt Dorothy placed the final touches on her first fancy dress the morning before the dance. Aunt Dorothy altered a pink bridesmaid dress her sister Kimyatta had worn. Because Katura's father didn't imagine his daughter attending dances, ingenuity came into play. Though she winced at the style of the original dress, her confidence in her aunt's sewing skills were boundless. What struck Katura most was the thought that she could look like a young *woman*. Aunt Dorothy's skills were certainly needed because this was not just any dress. She dared to wear Aunt Kimyatta's special plumage.

Years of admiring the women of her family as a child made her feel unsure of stepping into their shoes. Especially for the young girls, the aunts represented the finest women in the community. Everyone admired their feminine strength, dignity, intelligence and grace. These intrinsic qualities came in attractive packages. So she didn't only fear the sizable expectations of their characters, she also had to overcome insecurities about being beautiful and sexy. Her aunts wore clothes that her mother would never consider or her father allow. The children talked of scandals when they saw some of her aunts' clothes. The low-cut blouses and short skirts pushed the boundaries of her parents' conceptions of propriety. That's why she loved visiting her aunts. They weren't as strict as her parents. The 9th-grade formal allowed her to be a young woman distinct from her mother. Instead of living vicariously through her aunts' fancy wardrobes and busy social lives, she hoped to taste independence. So when she was told she'd leave for the formal from Aunt Dorothy's, she felt ecstatic *and* nervous.

Whenever Dorothy and her sisters went out, their children gathered downstairs to catch the women's re-creations of old fashions. Katura delighted in the fashion show, but the highlight always seemed to be Kimyatta. The other sisters deferred to Kimyatta and allowed her to polish the banister last. When she arrived, the children were as awed by Kimyatta's bodacious figure as the wide-eyed spouses who craned their necks to witness the spectacle. Kimyatta's rhythmic movements made her dress and all the eyes upon her dance. At the time, Katura couldn't make a T-shirt jiggle. How could she fill out the pared-down dress of her magnificent aunt?

But it was the dress that quieted Katura's insecurities. She loved the color. She called it "lady's" pink, because the tone was rich enough to show, yet soft enough to comfort. Weeks before trying on the dress, the idea of adorning it to make it her own instead of a miniature version of Kimyatta's made her more confident. She was nervous that evening, but the pink dress soothed her through the arduous hairdressing process.

At Aunt Dorothy's, early in the afternoon, the master bedroom and its adjacent bathroom were commandeered for the transformation. Her uncle was banished. When she entered the bedroom, she noticed the dress hanging from the bed's canopy. The cool color hit her like a swirl of cotton candy. Before she became completely stupefied, her aunt pushed her into the bathroom to bathe and wash her hair.

After a lightly perfumed body shower, two hair shampoos and a rinse, Dorothy blew out her hair with a handheld dryer and sectioned it for braiding. Aunty beckoned Kimyatta to help braid. Dorothy sat Katura in a chair facing the dress. The pink kept her rapt as the two women gossiped and worked their magic. After they completed the braids, the aunts slid in white and pink hairpins topped with delicate stars. After working on her hair for nearly three hours, Dorothy and Kimyatta helped her into undergarments and started makeup. They displayed expertise in their selection and application.

Dorothy said, "Color is everything."

However, it was not the makeup that transformed her. The women taught her the craft of becoming beautiful was a slow and deliberate process. As Dorothy compared different tones of lipstick, she described her first big date.

She said, "I was much older than you when I went on my first date." The two women laughed, and she recognized the emphasis placed on the words "first date."

"How old were you, Aunty?"

Dorothy replied, "I just turned eighteen, and I went out with Shaun Reid. He was a fine twenty-two at the time."

Kimyatta made the aside as she searched for perfume.

"He still *is* fine."

"… as frog hair," Dorothy said. "I remember, because the arrangement happened at my eighteenth birthday party. Shaun's parents asked my parents for permission to take me out."

Kimyatta jumped in. "That's right because all the sisters kept asking, 'Who's that stud of a man.'"

"That evening, I went through the same process you're

experiencing tonight."

"Who did *your* makeup?" Katura asked.

"Your Great-Aunt Bess, God bless her soul. She owned a salon down the street from here from the Depression until the day she died."

"She was all woman and a lady, too," Kimyatta said. "I never saw Aunt Bess outside without a fancy hat. People thought she was going to church when she was headed to the laundromat. She walked, talked, ate and drank like a lady. Never too much makeup. Not much more than lipstick and eye shadow— maybe a little blush. Aunt Bess believed too much hid natural beauty. She always reminded us too much junk clogs your pores, ruins your skin. If you use makeup, clean it off as soon as your event is done. And gently, with cotton balls and a makeup remover. Aunt Bess's prescription for beautiful skin was to drink lots of water, walk regularly and never place unwashed hands on your face."

"We learned everything from her."

Kimyatta paused, then recalled a story. "Remember when Aunt Bess taught us to walk properly?" She let out a big laugh.

Aunt Dorothy said, "You mean the peacock technique?"

Kimyatta said, "Make sure you clarify the difference between a pogo-stick trot and a peacock stroll."

"Stand up, Katura."

She stood.

"Let me see you walk."

She did a circuit around the room. They both shook their heads.

Dorothy said, "Now put on your shoes." She handed Katura the pink shoes, dyed to match the dress. Katura repeated the walk.

"Ouch," Kimyatta exclaimed. "Your feet hurt? Somebody's in

pain. It's either you or the shoes."

Katura's exaggerated steps were a caricature of her aunts' graceful movements.

Dorothy offered, "Don't knock anyone over. I'm glad you have two-inch heels. Maybe we should have dyed sneakers."

"It's not that bad. Quit teasing her, Dotty."

Kimyatta said, "You see, most girls don't know how to walk. You walk like a pogo stick when you should float like a peacock."

Katura giggled. Kimyatta grabbed her hips.

"These are feathers, and you are a peacock."

Dorothy interjected, "Aunt Bess used to take us to the zoo to watch the peacocks. You know how a peacock walks, right?"

Katura said, "I guess."

Dorothy said, "Peacocks are the proudest birds and they possess the most attractive feathers."

Kimyatta stated with Katura's hips in hand, "These are your feathers." She gave her hips a strong wiggle to loosen them and continued, "Peacocks walk slowly and carefully. They place each foot firmly on the ground. No step is made without care. Remember, the peacock's chin is held high. It doesn't need to look at its feet. A proud bird is confident in her steps. Look toward your destination. Occasionally grace spectators with your eyes to assess the terrain. Keep in mind the bird is not arrogant, but it refuses to be ignored. Its eyes briefly acknowledge onlookers to signal its presence. Once the space is claimed, the peacock struts."

Dorothy continued, "Don't forget about the feathers."

"The most important part of the walk is the feathers. Keep this in mind. Remember when you walk, the feathers are for show. They're not for fanning. Understand? Some unrefined women show their feathers by fanning. *Ladies* show their feathers discreetly. By walking. Nothing more, nothing less."

Kimyatta demonstrated the two strutting styles and asked Katura to follow. At first she wiggled too much. After a few walks, she caught the rhythm. Although she had only a few feathers, she used her small bouquet in concert with her walk. She quickly picked up the stride. After she mastered walking, Dorothy asked her to put on her dress. She powdered over her makeup to set it and covered the neck of the dress with a makeup drape so there'd be no smears on the "feathers."

Just as she put on the dress, Dorothy said, "Almost perfect!" Before she could rush over to the mirror, Dorothy grabbed her and touched up her eyeliner. After giving her a light kiss on her forehead, she said, "You're a perfect young lady."

Katura tiptoed over to the long mirror on the door and gazed in amazement. She could not believe her transformation.

She stood for about four minutes before she turned to say, "Thank you. I love you."

After they touched up any slips in the makeup or dress, the aunts went downstairs to announce the upcoming vision. After a few minutes of suspense, the women summoned her. Katura carefully placed her pink heels on each carpeted step. To her surprise, the family greeted her with smiles and camera flashes. Collective 'ahhs' sounded as she floated down. An uncontrollable smile flashed across her face, and she could see the looks that she gave her aunts on prior occasions on the waiting relatives. She heard the congratulations Dorothy and Kimyatta received and the pride they exhibited. The smiles her parents offered eased her final insecurities. While receiving accolades from a star-struck family, Kimyatta covertly tweaked her walk and posture. By the time Katura reached the end of the stairs, she felt she'd joined the ranks of womanhood in the family, all the way back to Great

Aunt Bess.

As she reached the bottom step, she heard Loren and his uncle pull up. Loren's Uncle Boo agreed to chauffeur Loren and Katura in his new, white Cadillac. The 9th-grade formal was the night that Loren and Katura planned in their own minds to be more boyfriend and girlfriend than just friends. As early as the 8th grade, Katura liked Loren. Images of them holding hands, eating meals, and talking filled her head. Suppressing these new feelings became increasingly difficult. Loren's dedication to school distracted her from her pubescent stirrings but fed their academic connection. She giggled when seeing him read a book, solve an equation, or complete an assignment. She enjoyed his dedication to seek out answers. Even when she knew a solution, she only dropped hints so he'd do his own work. She found pleasure in Loren's discussions on ideas. He finally began to enjoy school and Katura didn't want to stymie that. So she became a secret admirer and turned off her hormones, except in fantasy. Between classes, study sessions, or when frustrated from unrequited love, she thought of him.

With the exception of locker rooms, she was usually near Loren. She even became a cheerleader to keep herself busy. They were a classic American couple, even though he didn't realize it yet. She had everything except Loren's acknowledgement they were a couple. Everyone recognized them as a pair. Until that point, Katura swam in the speculation from students that the two were a match. However, scandals at such a tender age could ruin a lady's reputation. Besides, her parents wouldn't have approved. Therefore, she refuted innuendoes and commentary. Still, she wanted to feel more like a girlfriend. There was no doubt in her mind that she loved Loren, but his immaturity kept him from reciprocating. When she saw Loren step out of his uncle's car, it was a dream scene. Her African prince had rolled to her doorstep.

Loren looked his part. He wore black and a pink flower in his lapel to break the monotone and match her dress. She felt a sense of relief when she saw the corsage in his hand perfectly complemented her dress. As he walked into the house, her family's attention shifted to Loren. He noticed them gathering at the door and the buzz of excitement.

Her family swarmed around Loren. She noticed Loren's discomfort with the attention. Her family poked and prodded his suit, straightened his crooked tie, and plucked minutely visible loose threads. They took pictures of Loren in every pose. They even asked him to smile as he reached down to retie his shoe. His only quiet time was the five-minute meeting between Katura and her father. After taking several pictures of Loren and Katura, they got in the car and left.

The "first couple" arrived, providing the last strokes to the painting. Katura colored the scene pink. Loren was a gentleman. He parted the adoring crowd. Always a half step behind, Loren placed her in front and made sure she needed nothing. Every door was opened, every drink of punch brought speedily. She was the book he studied and observed. She spoke freely and often. They shared honestly, and for the first time, she didn't have to help. He did the work of making sure she was happy.

Throughout the night, they danced to heavy bass beats and tight harmonies. She had no idea he could dance. Loren did not *just* dance. He moved with her. Syncopated bodies make magic. Loren's steps followed hers, but he took the lead at the right times. An occasional hand on her hip told her he was with her. The lightest touches in the right places made her wonder. She was in teenage heaven in an old gym.

Then Clarence came.

"What's up, President Smooth?"

"Hi. Who did you come with?" Loren said drily.

"I came alone. Can't have a girl cramping my style."

"You mean no one said yes to you, and no one asked you," Katura said, hoping this might shoo him off.

Speaking to Loren, Clarence said, "Well, Katura did ask me, but I declined."

She corrected him. "I never asked you. Why don't you go talk to James? He looks like he needs a listener."

"James? He's no company and no dancer. Check this one out. I was dancing with Tiffany Copeland."

"Tiffany? Didn't she come with Bobby?" Loren asked

"And? You know Bobby and me. We trade. Anyway, I was dancing with Tiffany, and see James 'lead-foot' tripping over Woodstock."

Loren said, "James was dancing with knobby-kneed Woodstock?"

"I said trippin'. That fool couldn't move on time if a watch carried him. You've got to catch this."

A frustrated Katura asked, "Why don't you go play eye spy with James and Crissy?"

"You mean kickstand'and knobby knees?"

Before she could direct Loren to the next dance, Clarence grabbed him and said, "You've got to see this."

Clarence guided Loren to the other side of the gym. Arms crossed, Katura walked to Loren. By the time she reached him, the "rib" session had begun and James was snarling at Clarence.

Katura came in on a reply from James, "Why don't you rob a car or something and leave me alone?"

Clarence said, "Not before you steal some rhythm. Damn.

You dance like the whitest man in America or a white nigga from the 7th Ward."

"Why are you always calling me white? Move away."

"This school has about five white girls in it. How come you come to the formal with Woodstock? Where I come from, if it tastes, smells, and looks like chicken, it's chicken. If it dances, dates, and separates like whitey, it's got to be whitey."

After James saw Crissy remove herself from the circle that had formed, James uttered the ultimate fighting words. "Your momma dances like Charlie."

As soon as James talked about someone's momma, Loren jumped between the two. He placed his hands on each of their chests, but his arms were close to his body. Loren tilted his head as if he were bored with their conflicts. A small crowd moved closer as the climax approached. Most of the students grew disinterested with Clarence and James's feud. Students drifted back to dancing and socializing. Even teachers ignored the situation. It was the same tableau in a different scene—James on the right, Clarence on the left and Loren in the middle keeping the peace. Nonetheless, there were always idiots itching for a fight.

Someone said, "Did he say your momma dances like a white girl?"

A few yelled, "James called Clarence's momma a white girl."

Eventually, someone yelled, "Knock his punk ass out."

Loren tried pushing the two away from each other and said to Clarence, "Why do y'all have to always start something?"

Katura rushed to Loren's side to calm the trouble.

The boys' posturing was boiling over. They pressed on Loren's hands. The two faked a few punches and pushed each other. After the bravado cooled down, the rib session regenerated. Clarence projected his voice loud enough so all the students could hear.

"I know you're not talking about mommas. Your momma is so fat that she jumped in the air and got stuck."

The crowd let out a blast of laughter. Clarence was a master of the dozens. He preyed on students' weaknesses without restraint or mercy. Everyone knew that James' mother was obese. But no one talked about it. Clarence went for the jugular. He said, "Your momma's got more chins than a Chinese phone book." Even though they'd heard Clarence spout the same jokes before, the watchers clutched their stomachs in laughter.

Clarence continued, "I mean do you hug your mother or do you try to climb her wrist and call it a day."

Between each joke Clarence gauged his performance by the volume of the throng's laughter. After the last bomb Katura knew they were in for a long night.

Building on the last joke, Clarence said, "Now I know you're not black. If you were you would be the first black man to climb Mt. Everest."

The laughter boomed throughout the room and others noticed. James stood defensively as Clarence tore into his psyche.

"Let me stop before we get suspended and our parents have to bring us back to school. And we both know the school can't afford to build a landing pad on the roof."

Everyone saw scarlet seeping through James' brown skin. Katura felt so bad for him she asked Loren to make Clarence stop. Loren leaned over Clarence and whispered something in his ear. Clarence grinned in victory and satisfaction and started to leave.

Just as Clarence was about to back off, James told Loren, "Why do you hang around these ignorant niggers?"

Clarence said, "What did you say?"

Loren looked at James in disbelief. Clarence was genuinely angry now. Clarence had a history of not controlling his outbursts. But Loren's hand never left his chest. The crowd sensed the rage in Clarence and revived their interest.

Clarence said again, "What did you call me?"

Katura stood perplexed as Loren and James stared into each other's eyes for an uncomfortable stretch. Then he did the unspeakable. He broke the statue. Loren removed his hand from their chests and looked at Katura. She thought to herself, what was Loren doing? Loren grabbed Katura's hand and left the pair.

Clarence jumped in James' face and repeated, "What did you call me?"

Loren dragged Katura toward the door. They both knew the outcome. Clarence was going to kick James's ass. Before they left, they heard loud 'ooh's' and 'ahh's'. Teachers suddenly abandoned the punch bowl and moved to the circle. The music still played and students kept dancing. But the couple headed for Uncle Boo's car. Katura felt as if her pink dress turned blue as Loren told Boo they had to go home.

After Loren shut Katura's car door and got in, she asked, "Can we get something to eat?"

Loren said somberly, "I don't feel like eating."

"Do you want to walk around the Riverwalk?"

"We better get home."

"It's not late. Besides, Uncle Boo is with us." She spoke loud enough so Boo heard.

Loren turned his head, but kept quiet. "I'm sorry, Katura. I want to go home."

Loren said nothing for the rest of the ride to her house. They sat in the back seat as far apart from each other as possible. Loren stared out the window. She saw he was in pain and knew the fight had wounded him. It became a critical moment in his life and their relationship.

When they arrived at her house, he jumped out his door and ran to the other side to let her out. She got out slowly, then Loren spoke.

"I'm sorry the evening ended this way."

He left his hand on the door to signal it was time for her to go in. The porch light came on as she moved away from the car.

Loren walked her to the top of the stairs and her parents came out looking surprised.

Katura's mother said, "You're two hours early. Did something happen?"

They looked at each other and Loren said, "I have to go, Ms. Price. I will see everyone later."

Katura's parents said, "Get home safely, Loren."

Loren entered his uncle's car, and they left. To ease their concern, she told her parents what happened.

After a brief conversation, she walked to her room dejected, but afterward fell asleep. Instead of pleasant dreams, she woke to disturbing nightmares of verbal sparring and bloody fistfights.

Clarence's Turn

Loren and Carl were walking from practice while talking about the Penn Relays Carnival, the biggest track and field event in the country. The team was invitedtto participate. This was a major victory for the high school and a needed lift in the spring.

Loren saw Katura running furiously toward them while they talked. By the speed of her run, he knew something was amiss. When the details of her face became visible, it set off an alarm, but she was too exhausted to talk. Katura bent over huffing so hard he had to grab her shoulders to pull her up. Her torso heaved while she gasped.

"They got him."

He had no idea who she meant or for what. "Who and why?"

She spat out, "They got Clarence." Katura dropped her chin on her chest and said, "Clarence is in the hospital."

"What happened?"

After a few deep breaths she could speak normally.

"When we were walking to the store after school, the boys started ribbin' on each other. Clarence teased Skeeter about his homemade haircut and everybody laughed at him."

Carl asked, "Who was there?"

"Everybody... Mike, Steve, Junior, Clay, Bob, Kenny, everybody."

"Then what?"

"Clarence kept on ragging Skeeter about his haircut and he got mad."

Carl said, "So what? Skeeter can't beat Clarence."

"Skeeter pushed Clarence."

"What did Clarence do?" Loren asked, wondering how one push led to the hospital.

"Then Skeeter pushed Clarence again and Clarence told him stop or he would bust him up. Skeeter pushed him again and Clarence slammed him and pinned Skeeter on the ground by his neck."

Imitating Clarence's moves, Katura said, "Skeeter tried to get up but Clarence slapped him in the face and kept saying, 'What you goin' to do about it? What?' When Skeeter finally got loose, Clarence punched him in the mouth and said, 'I told you not to push me.'"

Katura still hadn't answered the seminal question. The two boys folded their arms waiting.

"OK, OK. After Clarence punched him, Skeeter ran down the street. Clarence chased him. Everybody ran behind. When they hit Bell's Drug Store, Clarence tripped Skeeter and he fell at the door. Before Clarence got another shot, Skeeter's older brother Peanut came out the store and started wailing on Clarence.

"First, Peanut was whoppin' Clarence. Peanut got him three good times in the face. But after they locked up, Clarence grabbed Peanut's pants cuffs and pulled Peanut down. Clarence punched Peanut in the face. Everybody was yelling. Then the Fiya Boyz came from across the street. All of them, even the older ones punched him in the face and one of them caught Clarence from behind. Chris's cousin Walt hit him so hard in the back of the head, Clarence was out!"

Carl looked amazed.

"Clarence landed on his face and you could see the blood spill on the concrete. Walt turned Clarence over and they kept kicking him in the face and ribs. People were screaming to stop, but nobody would help him."

Loren asked solemnly, "When *did* they stop?"

"Reggie came out the store and yelled that he'd called the police. After they got a few more licks in, they left Clarence for under the bridge to square off D.L. and Gemal with Chris and Walt. The gang followed, but Nekeisha, Cecily, and I waited by Clarence for the police. When no one showed, we went in the store to ask if Reggie had called. He said, 'No, I didn't. I hope they beat the shit out of each other and move away from my store.' Nekeisha went outside and called the police and ambulance on the payphone. By the time they came, everybody was gone but us three."

Loren was silent and fuming. Katura continued to describe the beating and several other people congregated for the tale. Michelle, Derek, and Corey joined the listeners.

Derek said, "Man, that's fucked up what the Fiya Boyz did." He turned to Loren and asked, "What we going to do about it?"

Corey said, "Fuck that president shit. Somebody's got to pay."

Derek said, "Loren, Clarence is *your* boy. This can't go down like this."

Carl asked, "Where is Clarence?"

"At Touro Infirmary."

Carl turned to Loren and said, "We got to see if he's all right. Let's call a taxi and go to Touro."

Derek said, "Hold up. What 's the payback plan?"

Carl said, "Let's go, man."

Derek snapped, "Shut up, Carl." He turned to Loren and said, "Yo, I hear that Peanut is hanging down by Manchu's."

Loren ended the conversation and said, "I'm not doing anything until I see Clarence."

Carl, Katura, and Loren walked toward his house. He heard Corey talk to Derek as they left.

"I told you he would pussy out. Loren ain't shit. I'm going to start calling him lame duck."

The sounds of their laughter dissipated as they separated, but the dissing lodged in Loren's head. He knew that Carl and Katura heard Corey. His focus shifted from Clarence's wellbeing to his reputation.

Reputation is very important in high school because a boy's status is tied positively or negatively to masculinity. In descending order boys were ranked on: sexual activity, athletic ability, fighting skills, appearance, intelligence, and a razor-edged tongue. High marks in all areas make a boy a contending alpha male.

Loren's rank was in the fair to good range. However, most of his fair to high marks were tenuous. For instance, they based a high percentage of boys' manhood on sexual conquests. While Loren didn't get any "pussy" at that time, people saw him as a person struggling to have sex with one of the finest, straightest girls in school. He got charity points for his efforts. More solid points came from athletics. However, football and basketball points ranked higher than track and cross-country. Fighting offered additional prowess. But, being an athlete meant he couldn't be associated with street brawls or he'd be suspended from his team, school or both.

The coaches made gym the last period, seventh, on athletes' schedules so they could leave school early for practice or competitions. By proxy they missed a lot of after-school fights. In addition, students thought to have futures outside of New Orleans fought less often than those who were likely to remain in the neighborhood. The community generally gave athletes and scholars the benefit of immunity, and Loren was both. Therefore, the loss or gain of status based on fighting ranked low for him. But Loren knew the demand for retribution for Clarence's beating was an exception to these rules.

People assumed Loren could tussle. This idea carried over from a few successful middle-school standoffs. His friends' reputations also contributed to his general respect. Their fight games were solid. And hanging with Clarence deflected physical threats because so many peers feared *him*. Loren suffered minor challenges, but no one expected him to raise his fists.

He could have dismissed Corey's challenge, but this time was different. Although he didn't hang with a crew, the same rules were in effect. If someone hurts your best friend, it was as if they hurt you. It was the unwavering law of adolescent retribution. A child realized "eye for an eye" never worked out well. However, they didn't live in a world of logic. School didn't teach justice, so they took simplistic routes— revenge.

Sometimes Loren believed the boys wanted these battles, not peace. Peace seemed too boring, so they traded it for violent encounters and Dark Ages justice. Corey lived by these laws and called out anyone who didn't participate. Adolescent males were quick to pull the "man" card if there were deviations from the rules.

While Loren was upset that Clarence was injured, he knew that everyone got a beat down some time. Clarence was long overdue. He had dished it out for a long time. Karma was not on his side, so why should Loren be? He honestly didn't feel much anger towards Peanut, Skeeter, or the other boys. He knew what goes around comes around. Loren had just developed a core group of friends that didn't fight. In fact, fighting had declined *in school.* Street scuffles continued, and Clarence took part.

Fighting was a sick, regular ritual. Students fought at parties, athletic events and along bus and streetcar stops. Loren's middle school experiences taught him how addictive violence was. No one ever thought there was enough action. Loren had tired of the self-destruction.

As Carl, Katura and he walked to Loren's house, his mood soured. He remained silent as Katura and Carl discussed the situation. He was fed up with the fight game. All he needed to know was if Clarence would live or die. He'd come so far, yet knew that others used fights as unhealthy ways to blow off steam. He wouldn't do it. If it meant losing friends, or his status, so be it.

Not long after Katura told him about the fight, he made his decision to pull back. He knew fighting Clarence's enemies wouldn't stop Clarence's pain, or subsequent fights, or Loren's growing desire to be disconnected from violence. He had one goal in mind: being president of the United States. He saw fighting as a hindrance to that goal. Loren dropped the blood sport, and he developed an affinity for discipline, political power, prestige, and respect. At some point after the Clarence fight, he felt that nothing could derail his dream. However, Loren knew that leaving violence meant potentially losing Clarence. School became a safe place. Loren wanted to rid the school of fighting the way he wanted to remove Mr. McClain. Since he overheard McClain and Simon he'd wanted to escape Mr. McClain, standardized tests, fighting and Johnson School. These were his main motivations to change.

However, Loren was deeply concerned with Clarence's health. He decided to give up his battle for male status, but needed to be sure Clarence was OK before he left for the Penn Relays. After he got home, Carl and he made plans to visit the hospital.

* * *

The receptionist looked at a card and said, "I'm sorry, but no one is allowed to see Clarence at the family's request. Only one name is on the visitors' list, so I have to ask that you see his parents if you want to be included."

Loren said, "There must be some mistake. We are cousins. I'm Loren and this is Carl, and we need to see him before we leave town tomorrow."

"Clarence's Aunt Bunny is the only one allowed to see him," the receptionist said flatly.

"Is she with him now? Do you think I can talk to her so I can get permission?"

"She left soon after he got a room."

As she looked at the card, Loren leaned over the counter to see if he could sneak a glimpse of what floor Clarence was on.

The receptionist pulled the card back and said, "The staff knows a gang beat up Clarence. The rules are in effect for his safety."

Loren said desperately, "Ma'am, I'm not in a gang, and I'm not trying to hurt him. I just want to know if he's OK. We leave for a track meet tomorrow and I want to know if he's all right."

The receptionist replied, "I'm sorry. I can't give out medical information. When you get back, check with his family. I'm sure he'll understand."

"Please. You can come with me. I just want to say goodbye."

"If I get a chance, I will let him know that Loren and Carl stopped by and you went out of town."

When Loren heard "If I get a chance," he knew she wouldn't do anything. All Loren could think was Clarence was going to disown him as a friend if he didn't see him. Loren's unwillingness to enact payback also threatened their friendship.

They made a few more efforts to find Clarence, but nothing worked. Carl and Loren left the hospital despondent, then went to Clarence's house. They knocked on his door for more than half an hour because Loren knew his grandmother was typically home all day. Loren finally guessed she was probably at Clarence's bedside.

Loren wrote a note for Clarence saying the team was scheduled to leave at 5:30 the next morning for Philadelphia, and that he would talk to him when they returned if possible. He placed the letter in the mailbox, and he and Carl returned to Loren's house.

Nothing went well for the next few weeks. That weekend was supposed to be *their* Penn Relays, but Loren ran a lackluster leg, which added to a disappointing showing. When Loren returned, he went to Clarence's house to see how he was doing. Again, no one answered the door. Clarence wasn't in school for three weeks and though Loren called and left notes, he got no response on how his friend was doing from the family or Clarence. Word on the street was that his uncle took him out of town to heal up. Someone else said his family got tired of his fighting and tried to put him in a boys' home.

During that period, Loren's peers repeatedly challenged him to fight one boy or another involved in Clarence's beating. Eventually, the challenges transformed into mumblings about Loren's loyalty and guts. However, many more students told Loren to stay out of it. Loren became one of the kids who was not supposed to fight. He had a future.

When Clarence finally came back to school, he was quiet and didn't broach the subject. Loren made several attempts to find out what happened to him and where he went. He sensed Clarence wanted the ordeal to be forgotten. For the most part, it faded away, just like the vanishing montage of daily brawls.

Alternative for the Alternative

I protested adamantly, "We can't suspend or expel every boy who gets into a fight!"

As chair of the suspension and expulsion committee, I presided over a board that heard cases initiated by the principal.

Dr. Sarnacola said, "Dr. Boyd, if we let Clarence get away with this, the rest of the students, and teachers, for that matter, won't respect us. We need standards."

"The standard is to teach every child, every day, not the ones that we like."

"We can't teach every child because Clarence is a terror. He disrupts our school environment."

"Terror? He's a 9th-grader who got into a fight. What about the bottom line: We don't get rid of kids for childish behavior? We teach them something more appropriate."

Dr. Sarnacola said, "We don't 'get rid' of children. But Clarence persistently gets into trouble. It's disruptive."

"Then we find ways to push him in the right direction. We have positive behavior specialists, social workers and counselors for a reason."

Dr. Sarnacola replied, "Some of our students need deeper mental health services. Clarence needs a different setting. We would like to refer him to an alternative school."

"Did you get the memo? The mental health services for children in New Orleans have waiting lists of weeks if not months. Alternative school? Charter schools are supposed to be alternatives to traditional schools that don't want to teach all children. Now we're talking about an alternative to the alternative? I know Clarence. He's an immature boy who's had poor role models."

"I work with him, and the teachers work with him. He is out of control. You're not here every day."

"Clarence has got into two fights this year. If there are no weapons or drugs involved, then you suspend him, and assign him the services we provide. Hold a school-wide assembly and have him apologize. Do something different, but we are not expelling Clarence."

"With all due respect, I'm supposed to be principal of this school."

"With all due respect, we have an expulsion committee to prevent things like this from happening. Remember this is New Orleans. You know what happens to boys who are expelled. They're out of school with nothing constructive to do. Eventually, they see judges. This is not about usurping authority. This is about giving kids a chance."

There was a long silence. As if no other committee members were in the room, I said, "We've made our decision."

How is Your Grandmother Doing?

"How's your grandmother doing? I haven't seen her in a while." Loren tried to make small talk during a quiet walk from the bus stop after school.

Clarence said glumly, "She's not doing so well."

"What's going on?" As soon as he uttered those words, he tried to recall when he'd last seen Clarence's grandmother. It must have been months— an eternity for friends not to see each other's live-in relatives. Like most of Loren's friends, Clarence was raised by someone other than his mother. They lived a five-minute bike ride away from the rest of their crew.

In the past, Clarence always invited the neighborhood brood over to chill. Ms. Redman was the consummate hostess. Cookies were always as warm as the stories she told the gang of children missing nuclear parents. It seemed like the neighborhood grandparents more often took turns feeding and raising them. Occasionally, when Loren was too hungry to wait for dinner at home, he scurried over to Clarence's for a change of taste. The Redmans' house was always his first choice if his mom worked late or he got home early. Clarence's grandmother welcomed him like another grandson.

As they walked, Loren kept trying to remember the last time

he was in Clarence's. He felt embarrassed. He'd broken some unwritten rules. Clarence was one of his closest friends and he hadn't missed him. Loren knew Clarence was disappointed but reluctant to confront him after the fight that landed him in the hospital. Loren dreaded a declaration of disrespect with each passing step. He thought about the time he'd spent with books, running and Katura. Clarence had been written off his schedule. How had Loren become so insensitive and ungrateful to Clarence and Queen Mama?

They affectionately called Ms. Redman Queen Mama. It was a moniker she accepted. Their perfunctory greeting was, "Looking good today, Queen Mama." She smiled softly each time they used the name. She blushed, saying, "Now you know to call me by my right name."

They knew not to disrespect their esteemed sage of the block. However, as kids, they discovered the value of playful flattery with elders. Their teasing was a token of appreciation. Ms. Redman deserved her title. She gained it partly because of age; she was the eldest woman on Franklin Avenue. She was a mother and a lady. While some mothers' clumsy manners embarrassed their children, Ms. Redman's grace established a finer tone. Despite Queen Mama's stature, Loren never heard her brag except of course when she talked about her two sons, whom she obviously loved.

In many ways, Clarence was a prince among serfs. Loren never heard Queen Mama call Clarence anything but "Baby": "Good job on that report card, Baby." "Baby, can you run to the store for me?" "Baby, how was your day at school?" Clarence chafed at his pet name, especially in the presence of the guys. "Baby, Baby, Baby" all day was tough on a young man in front of friends. She always told the boys to wear modesty like a suit of armor. At the time, Loren thought it a bit of hypocrisy that she called Clarence "Baby." Expressing love for a child is a form of pride a mother can't deny. This was especially true when children made it to college.

Her other grandson, Billy, had made that grade. Queen Mama's pride was on display like an Easter bonnet as she mentioned Billy's accomplishment.

But she was never condescending with her joy over the first in her family to attend a university. Neighborhood etiquette allowed this exception. Parents customarily bragged unapologetically over major educational benchmarks. Clarence and the gang definitely valued Queen Mama's praise, for it was indirectly their first push toward the unimagined world of college. Ms. Redman's sincerity equaled her pride, and listeners realized the boasting was blended with love.

Although she'd never set foot on a campus, she knew everything and everyone that was on Billy's. Queen Mama read the materials her grandson's college sent to the parents in great detail and with passion. She spoke as if she and the college's president were on a first-name basis. For the longest time Loren believed they were. His most vivid memories of her were of how she searched high and low for a hat appropriate for Billy's graduation: "I have to find a peacock raised on sugarcane for hat feathers sweet enough for that precious moment."

As soon as Billy left their tiny community, Clarence and his grandmother became inseparable. He walked with her regularly to the park and library. They caught taxis to the grocery store and back home. Clarence strived to make Queen Mama happy, and she responded by giving him more responsibility and freedom. "Baby" was a young man. Clarence held up his end of the bargain by coming home after school to finish homework and returning from parties at a reasonable hour. He chose not to drink and smoke out of respect for her. The only stain on his record was fighting, ignited by the slightest remark against his grandmother. Any comment was resolved quickly during or after school. Playing the dozens with Clarence meant you had to remove "Your Momma" jokes from the session.

Loren did not talk for several blocks after passing Bell's Drug Store, the dealer's spot, and Dave's Barbershop. They got props from local hustlers, basketballers, and school friends along the way. At another street, they said hello to Zach, the corner drunk, and gave him change. A few seconds later, the driver of the 7 o'clock Franklin Ave. bus beeped her horn at them. Finally, they spoke to the neighborhood bully, Janero, who was suspended for fighting a few days earlier.

Loren said to Clarence, "Let's go to your house."

"I really don't feel like it," Clarence said.

Loren said, "I want to say, 'Looking good today, Queen Mama.' She always laughs when she hears that."

"Mama has been sick a while, Loren," Clarence said dourly.

An awkward pause stalled their conversation.

"It's getting worse? Is she going to be OK?" Loren asked worried.

"They say she has dementia, and she needs to find a nursing home."

"Man, you just told me she was getting a little confused!"

"She can't remember people or things, except from decades ago. She forgets our address, gets lost walking in the neighborhood and doesn't recognize people she knew. She's scared, too."

"I didn't know it was that bad."

"I noticed her forgetting and confusing names last year, but I remember when I knew something was wrong."

Clarence continued, "I was sitting at the kitchen table after a late-night hangout with you. As I expected, Mom came down the stairs and started talking. I thought she was going to ask where I had been and give me the 14-point grilling. I was so used to the routine that I must've put the words together for her. She didn't make sense. I told her I came from your house, and your mother let us watch a movie. Her response was wack. I ignored it and went to bed. Over the next couple of weeks I noticed Mom did this all the time. The jibberish became crazier. I came home late from school one day, and she was in the basement opening picture boxes and throwing her photos on the floor."

"Were they the pictures of all the folks in the old neighborhood?" Loren asked.

"All the pictures of our families were everywhere. You know how she loved everybody's grandparents."

"I remember she had a picture of Carl's grandmother playing cards and drinking beer."

"Loren, don't forget your folks were in those pictures too. The only time I saw my mom and my pa happy together was in her pictures."

They walked silently a few blocks, passing the po-boy shop and check-cashing store. Loren didn't know what to say. Although he wasn't completely aware of Clarence's grandmother's state, he understood his friend was distressed. Loren found it hard to express sympathy due to his male "suck it up" training. Words that could start tears were as taboo as crying. Instead of stumbling through that minefield, they walked silently, digesting Clarence's disclosure. Like children clutching their parents' legs at the sight of strangers, they were afraid to face these complex emotions.

Clarence digressed to his comfort zone.

"Do you think I could join the cross-country team?"

Loren was caught off guard.

"Why?"

"I need to get my mind off this."

"I thought you said cross-country is a white sport."

"I can maintain in the wintry wonderland."

"Can you run?" Loren asked, unsure if Clarence had the skills.

"You put one foot in front of the other. I've been doing it all my life."

"It may be a little too late," Loren warned sincerely.

"I see how people treat you. Coaches are sweating you. Everyone on that team seems like they're getting somewhere with their lives. It's been hard for me, Loren. I'm stuck helping Mom, and it's getting to me."

"Yo. Running is not going to make your problems go away. But what about the rest of your family?" Loren asked, thinking about duty and responsibility.

"You know my cousins couldn't come back. The hospital she was supposed to go to is closed. We tried to get her in a nursing home that was supposed to open up last week, but they said next month."

"How are you doing all this, man?"

"I love Mom, and she's all I have, but she is fading fast. Katrina is killing her. She won't be around. I have to make plans. I don't even remember the last time she remembered my name. She calls me Billy when she speaks at all."

For one of the few times in his life, Loren was in a conversation with a male peer that didn't end with a joke or a punch. This was real. He listened intensely because Clarence hadn't been the most sensitive person. But he was sincere, so his words sank in. Loren stood frozen as he watched Clarence's hands wipe over his face, neck and finally fall to his sides. Loren figured he was wiping away tears.

"I'll talk to Mr. D. tomorrow. Bring your practice clothes to school."

* * *

As they walked silently Loren knew they were going to see Queen Mama.

With a small grin, Clarence said, "So how does it feel, Loren?"

Not sure what he meant by the question, Loren frowned and asked, "What do you mean, 'How does it feel?'"

"How does it feel being Mr. President everywhere you go?"

"I guess it feels good."

Clarence stopped and looked at him skeptically. Clarence screwed up his mouth. Loren was uneasy with the mood change.

He reevaluated his statement and said, "It feels damn good."

They kept walking slowly as Clarence said, "Promise me something, Loren."

"What's that?"

"Make sure you remember me when you become president for real. There are a lot of people counting on you."

"What do you mean? You're going to be in my cabinet."

"Sounds big. Just remember a brother."

Clarence's signature stone cold demand for loyalty assured Loren that he had learned to cope with his family situation, and his stoic demeanor masked the worries he faced. Clarence seemed unbreakable— the epitome of manliness.

Again they saw the same folks in their same positions on porches and stoops as they returned home. Along the way to Clarence's house the conversation became shallow. They discussed new music and which team had the best chance to win the basketball tournament.

Then they came to the bottom of his block. The view reminded Loren of where they were headed. He developed a slight knot in the middle of his chest, which grew as they got closer.

Clarence seemed about to discuss something that he had kept to himself for months. Loren was about to see the subject of his secret, feel the motivation for keeping it secret, and to revisit someone he hadn't seen for months.

Loren tried to make small talk to avoid feeling anything. He sensed the strain Clarence felt. It was something he needed to share, for the burden was too much. Loren realized that with all the adversity they'd faced in their lives, they still hadn't considered questions of nonviolent death. They compartmentalized shootings and other violent crimes in a callous part of their brains. This was different. They began to see how finite their lives were notwithstanding the fortresses they built around their hearts and minds. Walking closer to Clarence's house opened an awareness that would redirect their lives forever. Loren was fortunate to make this journey with his friend. For months, Clarence dealt with this ordeal home alone.

They approached the same front door Loren had entered a thousand times before, but the setting was less familiar. The white door had been recently repainted by an amateur, and fingerprints blemished the typically clear glass— a sign Queen Mama was not in charge. Loren felt anxious, though Clarence seemed composed. He opened the door and Loren followed inside. The hallway wasn't fresh as he remembered it. The house was neglected and its disorder drained some of Loren's energy.

Clarence was a step ahead of Loren, which provided a shield. He gave him a pained look and paused a few moments. Clarence's reluctance to enter forewarned Loren of what he had to face as he moved reluctantly behind him. From the living room they saw into the dining room where Clarence's grandmother sat at the dining room table. He moved behind Loren, placed his hand gently on his shoulder, looked toward Ms. Redman and said, "Queen Mama, you have a visitor."

Loren took a constricted breath that rattled in his throat. He didn't remove his gaze from the safety Clarence's face provided as his friend pushed him toward her.

Loren said, "Hi, Queen Mama. How are you? Long time no see."

She seemed to look through Loren. There was a long pause.

Then Queen Mama said, "I saw a little kid under my chair. Did you get him?"

Loren was taken off guard. He didn't know how to respond. He said, "It's me, Loren. How are you?"

"You look so different. You're getting tall. I thought you were Billy. Can you take that boy home so he doesn't make someone trip and fall? And Billy, get me a ginger ale."

Clarence went into the kitchen and grabbed the soda from the kitchen table. Queen Mama carefully took the can from him and took delicate sips from the straw.

Clarence said, "This is Loren— Mr. Pres. You remember Loren, right?"

With a pleasant laugh of assurance she said, "He looks so familiar. Did you see the boy?"

Loren replied, "No, ma'am."

She continued to ask delusional questions that Loren could not make up responses to.

Clarence sensed that Loren was dazed by what he heard, and tapped him on the shoulder.

"Are you all right?" he asked.

Surprised by the touch, Loren said, "I am OK. I guess."

Clarence began a series of duties that seemed routine. He heated up a plate that his relatives made for Queen Mama. He cleaned up small living room messes that she would never have missed in the past.

"Loren, it's OK. See, she's smiling. She's just confused."

Even though Loren could barely look, Clarence carried on a delightful conversation with her.

"How was your day today, Mom?"

He raised his voice, pretending volume would help her understand.

"I said, how was your day today? I see Aunt Bunny made you macaroni. I am so glad she did, because I have to hang with President Loren."

Clarence looked over at Loren and grinned in thanks.

"Queen Mama, can you say hi to Loren? I said, can you say hi to Loren?"

He turned to Loren and said, "She is better in the mornings. She gets tired late."

Clarence leaned close to Ms. Redman's ear and asked loudly, "Mama, Mama, say hi to Loren before he leaves."

Ms. Redman did not respond.

"Did you watch your favorite TV shows today? You have to tell me after Loren leaves."

Clarence was a different person at home. Loren never saw Clarence so selfless. Why was he so mean in school? Loren was confused. There was such a disconnect between Clarence's home and school life. The impetuous violence that characterized Clarence in school was a mask that hid his distress over his grandmother's illness and their declining relationship. Loren saw a mature, kind, and generous Clarence— one distinctly different from his school image. After watching Clarence converse with his grandmother, Loren kept asking who was his real friend: the school bad boy or this patient, diligent nurse.

Clarence finished one chore after another as Loren considered the gravity of his situation. Occasionally, Clarence asked him gently to move.

"Is there anything I can do?" Loren asked after Clarence fluffed a pillow.

"Get me on that cross-country team."

"Clarence, your ma and you need more than a cross-country team. I think she needs a home nurse or the hospital. Your Aunt and you can't do this alone. I think it's brave you've tried, but you're beat down, man."

Clarence looked over at Loren, then hung his head. Loren saw there were tears in his eyes.

Too Proud to Beg for Change?

Going into the second school year, the state opened up the school supervision flood gates in order to convert pre-storm failing schools that were run by the New Orleans Public School District to independently managed charter schools. The state encouraged non-profit providers with the capacity to turn around failing schools and keep successful ones going. Although the storm pounded the university financially, if there was ever a test for a college of education to prove its mettle, this was it. If we couldn't run a few schools, then our teaching theory was useless in the real world. The deans and the president accepted the challenge. At the request of the state and local community, the university developed a network of four schools. In addition, dozens of non-profits applied for school takeovers and the state willingly surrendered. Upstart non-profits citywide were entrusted with charter schools. The conversion from traditional board-run schools to charters left the elected New Orleans Public School Board with as few schools as the university. Within a few years more than 70 percent of the children were educated in independently run, publically financed schools, and the state seemed poised to charter them all.

"Anything but the School Board" became a slogan for the

chiefs of the recovery. However, the heads of the various recovery committees did not know how to transform the beleaguered district. As the state converted and opened more charter schools, local philanthropists and the business community recruited and welcomed national education service providers to the Crescent City. National models were implemented as the innovation the city's leaders coveted. Innovation was not just a buzzword for the architects of recovery. The people stranded outside the Convention Center and Superdome a few months prior showed the rawest evidence of why we needed change.

My thoughts always return to the immediate aftermath of Hurricane Katrina. Thousands of thirsty, hungry humans waited outside the Convention Center in hopes of getting basic needs satisfied. Meaningless items that had become too burdensome to carry were strewn across empty spaces on cracked, black-topped streets. Big mamas sat among discarded water bottles, dirty sheets, and grocery store carts. Elderly women in dirty, oversized, sweat-drenched T-shirts lay on concrete steps, too tired and weak to stand, and help from the government didn't come in time for some.

I sat quietly, hundreds of miles away and watched, hands over mouth, as black people suffered and died. I realized most of those stranded were victims of the former educational system. The emotional pain associated with viewing the atrocities could not compare to the educational tragedies preceding them and, of course, the experience of living or dying through them. Pictures told the story of why we needed something new. Gap-toothed grimaces from obese diabetics in old wheel chairs confirmed who was left behind. As I watched, shame overwhelmed me, and my gut twisted. I could also hear the critics of welfare queens, government dependents and high-school dropouts. I knew the bootstrap backlash would emerge to whip black people. That backlash would arrive by way of messiahs who would deliver New Orleans from itself, educational failure and wayward culture.

Saviors of education started their descent into New Orleans when the camera lenses turned on "looters," gangs and opportunists. From AWOL cops to Wal-Mart raiders, chaos sported black faces. The use of the term refugee emerged. The cameras showed behaviors but left context behind. For every mindless thief who lifted a television, useless in a city without electricity, there were hundreds seeking food, water and clothing. Yet few could distinguish looters from survivors. I indiscriminately judged. Someone was to blame. I kept thinking, how does it come to people suffering and lying dead in the streets of one of America's most cherished, historic cities? I looked for help to arrive for the displaced people outside the Convention Center. It came way too late.

Too many poor black people did not have the resources that a quality education could have provided. Too many did not have the material goods or discretionary income to escape an impending danger. Families did not receive an education basic enough for them to get out of harm's way. New Orleans needed new ideas that would prevent smaller man-made tragedies from leading to the crescendo of disasters immediately following the breaches in the levees. Reformers did not believe that New Orleans' systems had the people or incentives to change on their own. Takeover became morally acceptable in the face of such suffering.

Transforming old school cultures became the goal in which morally justified takeovers received national and local financial support. In a city where locals were typically preferred and expected, national foundations seeded their human capital. The quickest way to change culture is to change people. Principals, school leaders and other practitioners sought programs that would locate quality teachers who could alter expectations and outcomes. Consequently, non-profits filled school staffs with outsiders.

The state ceded hundreds of contracts to non-profits, consultants, teacher training programs and companies hoping to find innovators in and outside of the classroom. The contractors would often provide touristy visits to the city. Schools started budgeting for itinerant workers. Schools paid a premium to find and bring talent into the city, albeit for a relatively short time. Direct investments to organizations whose mailing addresses fell outside the metro area made it difficult to determine who would ultimately benefit from these relationships. New Orleans proved long before the storm that it could draw consultants to the region simply using Bourbon Street as a carrot. But who showed up?

Innovation is about listening to new voices, not necessarily to people from other places. New Orleans heard the shrill pro/anti charter debates for so long that we forgot there were locals who had contributions to make. However, the reform movement had a tendency to limit new voices to those from the outside. I arrived before the storm, and I could easily climb onto the reform wagon. I knew that people trusted me partially because I was an outsider. I got a seat at the table. However, I'd like to think I brought a new voice.

New Orleans direly needed compassion and cooperation. The urgency of education reform should have been driven to give those trapped outside the Convention Center the education, skills, jobs and trust to control their destinies. At the very least, captains of industry and philanthropy could have incentivized benefits to those most likely to stay beyond short, self-aggrandizing band-aid jobs.

New Orleans became a test site, which profited the city in the short term and let workers off the hook whose tendency or plan was to leave once their service, pity or contracts were exhausted. Imposing educational changes that improve the community at large requires a framework that rewards long-term commitments to the community. We needed good ideas, but we also needed people to bring them to fruition and stay the course afterward. Change without community input spells danger and failure.

From the dramatic demographic shifts in the teaching corps of several schools, it became apparent that school leaders operated under a theory of action that assumed developing new school cultures required outside teachers. The fact that many of the New Orleans teachers were not being absorbed in the faculties of new charters suggested a theory of *improving by replacing* was at work. New schools hired few if any Orleanians.

The local black newspaper, *The Louisiana Weekly*, showed the racial and physical demographics and credentials of new teachers in the area, and which schools employed them. Thirty percent of the teacher population in New Orleans comprised first-year teachers primarily trained by the TPP program and working in School Horizon incubated schools. Almost all of the new teachers were white and 70 percent left the field and/or the city after two years. *The Weekly* highlighted schools like Sojourner Truth, which didn't have a single black teacher. After the reports seeped into the city's discourse, a slew of responses came from school reformers, who explained that if we eliminated teachers who taught the bottom 10 percent of failing schools, then the system could have a chance at improving. Martha Hagadorn of New Horizons and Crescent City Prep Principal Brian Rice became the spokespersons for such changes.

Martha, Brian and I accepted an invitation from the black talk radio station WBLK. My schools showed the same general demographics as prior to the storm, so I felt no need to have to defend them. Binky Smith conducted the interview, which initially went as I expected.

Smith asked, "If kids are improving academically, then why does the race of the teacher matter?"

Martha replied, "Reform has to be about the kids. Everyone keeps talking about adult issues. More and more students are passing the state exam. We are giving kids a chance. The graduates who commit to the Teacher Plus Program are some of the smartest young adults from around the country. All you have to do is be smart and have a big heart."

Brian jumped in.

"We don't go in saying, 'Let's find white teachers; they're better.' That report suggests we are discriminating."

I replied, "Student outcomes have to be a priority, but if a school shows a pattern of not hiring people of a certain racial, ethnic or regional background, then that's a problem. Talent comes in all shapes, sizes and colors and locally as well as from elsewhere. If our teacher pools are limited, then students lose the benefits of diversity."

Binky jumped on the point. "Aren't any of the former NOPS teachers talented? How many teachers do you currently have from the old system?"

I said, "Of the experienced teachers in the system, about 70 percent had experiences in NOPS."

Binky then asked Brian the same question.

Brian said, "I don't have any at this time. We had several, but they were not aligned with our reform strategies."

"What does that mean?" Binky asked.

"Our curriculum and the way we teach are so different from how it was done in the past. Lots of former NOPS teachers try, but they can't seem to switch gears. It's not about black or white. It's about whether or not you can change."

Binky then said, "We received several reports that the teachers are not culturally competent. What does that mean?"

I replied, "Teachers have to know the whole student and that means the sociopolitical context, race, ethnicity, as well as the educational levels of students and parents. Teachers have to know this so they will know how lessons are relevant to students in a real-world context, so lessons are reinforced outside school walls."

"Do you think some of the teachers are not culturally competent?"

Martha responded, "TPP and New Horizons provide all of our new teachers with a multicultural course the summer before they start working. We also bring in aspects of the culture we think they should appreciate."

"Like what?"

"We bring local experts who can discuss the Mardi Gras Indians as well as the social aid and pleasure clubs."

Sensitive to "culture in a can," I interrupted, "It takes time to become aware of your surroundings. We can't just limit culture to Carnival. That's what outsiders do all the time in New Orleans, and that's one of the reasons why outsiders can be ignorant of students' lives. Culture is also about literature, science, visual arts and traditions that fall outside of the realm of entertainment. That's why I never like the idea of importing college graduates and putting them to work with so little saturation. Graduates have spent four years in a specific location where they've learned a broader landscape than just their collegiate institution. Why not encourage graduates to teach in the area where they became members of the community? Trust me, there is a low-performing district close to every college or university. We don't have to import so many people to the city. We have seven universities here that should be able to provide culturally competent teachers."

Brian rushed in. "Why do we find ways to limit talent? When the Saints want players they search for people from anywhere and everywhere."

I said, "NFL teams don't just take people in college who are in great shape. All of them essentially majored in football in college. If we were hiring folks from all over the country who were trained to be teaching professionals, I wouldn't have a problem. Kids teaching in the TPP program were not in education programs. Most have no teaching experience. And you're telling me there isn't any local black graduate who wants to go into teaching? It's just not optimal, efficient or sustainable to recruit people because they have good hearts and minds. We have a rubric for everything else, why can't diversity and commitment be included in how we hire?

Binky asked, "You all are movers and shakers in the reform world. What are we going to do with a school like Armand Lanusse?"

Brian replied quickly, "As soon as I heard the story of how a security guard handcuffed a child to a chair, I immediately drafted a plan to serve the needs of that school. I plan to present the plan to the Treme Community."

Binky swooped in.

"Are you planning to take over Armand Lanusse?"

Brian said, "I am going to present what we have done with Prep since working at the Joseph Rainey site. School achievement has gone up thirty points since taking over the school. As you know, all schools are running out of space as more and more families return. I think the Treme community deserves a quality provider to fit the new facility. I even purchased a home in Treme. I am committed to serving kids and my neighborhood."

Before Brian could finish his statement, the call-in line lit up like a Christmas tree.

One caller said, "I'm tired of these white folks serving us steak on a dirty platter. You know this deal was done a long time ago. This stinks to high heaven."

The next caller said, "I'm a parent at Armand Lanusse, and that principal they got in there now gots to go. My child is not getting a good education, and I don't care who comes in Armand Lanusse just as long they can do better than what we got now."

Binky said, "Thanks, caller. We have our good friend Baba Karim on line three. Baba Karim, you have something to say. I know you do."

Baba Karim replied angrily, "No one consulted Baba Karim about this. I refuse to let carpetbaggers teach *our* children. These are our children. They don't care about *our* children. That Brian boy been here two years and now they are calling him the education czar. He can barely control what he got now. How is he going to come over here? We will not let these people in Treme. Over my dead body."

For the next twenty minutes until the segment ended, the focus shifted to Brian and his proposal for Armand Lanusse.

Logan Chicken is Too Bad to Eat

I received a call from Ms. Pringle, principal of our K-8 school, Elysian Terrace Charter, informing me that the Logan Chicken Factory delivery lady had arrived. The Logan delivery person was Cassandra Constance, mother of Brandy Stokes, who was a 180-lb. 4th-grader. The school dietician advised the principal and Ms. Constance that Brandy needed a special diet because of her weight.

The 9-year-old told her mother that she did not like the food, so Ms. Constance brought Brandy a two-piece, spicy Logan chicken meal around lunchtime, daily. Principal Pringle would not allow the meal, but Ms. Constance found a way to get it to her daughter. She stuck them in her schoolbag, or Brandy sneaked outside and met her mother for the contraband. Ms. Constance arranged meetings at different places during the day for counseling or parent-teacher conferences simply to drop off the meals.

Brandy's physical education teacher placed Brandy in an intramural volleyball league to get her extra exercise. But Ms. Constance brought chicken to volleyball practices and games. By any means necessary, Brandy got her chicken. This sleight-of-hand game occurred for months. By spring break, intercepting

Ms. Constance became a nearly impossible nuisance. At wits' end, Ms. Pringle asked me to intervene.

I was driving nearby when I received the call. As I approached the school, I saw a relatively thin, attractive woman holding a bag of Logan's chicken debating with Ms. Pringle. I got out of the car and could hear Ms. Pringle's polite tone start to fade.

Before I could introduce myself, Ms. Pringle said, "Let me introduce you to Dr. Boyd, who will confirm our food plan for your daughter."

Ms. Constance turned to me sourly and said, "How are you Dr. Boyd? I am just trying to bring lunch to my daughter."

"I understand your daughter's on a special diet."

Ms. Constance replied, "She says the food is nasty."

"Well, we have a dietician working to help your daughter. We have to work together to help Brandy practice good eating habits.

"She's not happy."

"The food is designed to meet her nutritional needs."

Ms. Constance's volume shot up, "She's not eating anything. So what's the point if she's starving?"

"She has meals that are available for her."

An irritated Ms. Pringle interrupted and said slowly, "Brandy eats the food."

Ms. Constance replied quickly, "She says it's nasty. You wouldn't eat that food."

"I would eat the food, if my health demanded it. We want Brandy to be healthy, don't we?"

"You's a lie. You never tasted that food."

I started to become irritated, but calmly said, "What do you mean by nasty? That bag of chicken has excess calories and fat beyond what the dietician recommends for Brandy, or for that matter, anybody, healthy or not."

"I told you she doesn't eat."

Ms. Pringle interrupted again, "Brandy doesn't miss breakfast or lunch."

She punctuated her statement with twisted lips.

I thought to myself on this glorious, spring afternoon that we couldn't be fighting over a greasy chicken dinner. Right before I could think of something else to say, Ms. Constance signaled to a pickup in the parking circle. A tall, muscular, brown man dressed like a laborer came over.

Ms. Constance looked me directly in the eye and said, "This is Brandy's father, Brandon Stokes."

I extended my hand and said, "You came to parent orientation this year."

He smiled briefly and said, "Yeah, I was there."

I'd guessed correctly.

Ms. Pringle reached out and said with a level of familiarity, "How are you Mr. Stokes?"

He replied as if ashamed to be standing there. "Hey."

Ms. Constance continued, "We come all the way down here every day to bring Brandy lunch, and all y'all do is tell us no. Y'all say we can make our children's lunch, but for Brandy it ain't so. My baby deserves a lunch I can bring."

I asked, "You're coming from work?" and looked at Mr. Stokes.

"Yes, we come from work. Our baby's got to eat."

"So you both take off work to bring Brandy a lunch she doesn't need?"

Ms. Pringle strained to repeat, "Brandy eats our food every day."

Taking the kettle off the burner, I said, "I can tell you love Brandy. It has to be difficult taking off work daily to bring

Brandy food."

I placed my hand on Ms. Constance's shoulder and said, "I know you want her to lose the weight."

I looked her husband up and down. He was a working man.

"I don't mean to be mean to you or Brandy, but I'm guessing your 6-foot-tall husband weighs 180 pounds."

There was a minute of silence.

With what looked like sadness in his eyes he said softly, "I weigh 185."

"And Mr. Stokes is a working man who exercises regularly. Brandy is a little girl who can't really enjoy being a child. She can't run or play like her schoolmates. Do you know they make fun of her? Food is her comfort and it's ruining her."

Before her mom could reply, I said, "She resembles you. Don't you want Brandy to look healthy and attractive like you?"

Ms. Constance mumbled "Yes."

Lifting my hand off her shoulder, I continued, "That chicken won't get Brandy where she needs to be. She's going to be injecting insulin if we're not careful. And I can tell your husband is tired of taking off work to come down here."

Mr. Stokes looked up for a moment.

Gaining some momentum I said, "I know it hurts when your child says she's hungry. Doesn't it?"

Indignantly she replied, "Hell, yes. I love my daughter, and I will do anything for her."

I said, "Then help her get fit. We can help you deal with her anxiety that comes with the loss of this crutch. We'll have our social worker help you. Imagine how happy she can be with friends and activities instead of food."

We paused for a few good seconds, and I said, "But we can't have you bring Logan's chicken or any food that doesn't fit her diet on the premises. I hope we are clear."

Ms. Constance reluctantly said, "OK." She exhaled deeply, but I could see relief in the father's face. I reached for the bag of chicken and tossed it in the garbage. After our goodbyes, I watched them drive away.

A few days later, Ms. Pringle called to tell me that Ms. Constance transferred Brandy to another charter school closer to her home. I never went to Logan's chicken for a meal again.

Haunted Schools

Mr. Simon, Loren, Katura and other members of the newly formed Johnson Debate Team were on their way back from a weekend tournament in Bogalusa, La. Mr. Simon drove the children in a university van. He and his crew of seven were approximately an hour away from their 9 p.m. estimated arrival Saturday night. Mr. Simon was piqued by conversations he overheard between Loren, who sat next to him, and Katura in the back seat.

Katura said, "I don't like going to that haunted school late at night."

"If you're scared, call the police."

"Those ghosts don't scare you?"

"Nobody's going to hurt you."

"You better walk with me to my locker, Loren."

"Stop being a wuss."

The back and forth continued regarding "ghosts" in the school. Confused at what he heard, Mr. Simon interrupted.

He asked, "What do you mean, ghosts?"

Katura said, "Those white teachers are in the building late at night. They scare me."

Nonplussed, Mr. Simon pressed her.

"What are you talking about?"

"The teachers in the upstairs school stay late at night."

"You're calling the white teachers ghosts?"

"Yeah, when we come back from these trips, they're always there."

Loren said, "When we come from cross-country meets they're upstairs still working. They must sleep up there."

Almost all of the teachers at Crescent City Prep came from the Teacher Plus Program, which recruited college graduates into teaching positions in inner-city schools. In exchange for a two-year commitment, new graduates got a job, loan forgiveness, and an opportunity to help transform public education. Most of the participants were white graduates of selective colleges around the country.

TPPers developed a reputation for working 10- to 12-hour days. What they missed in classroom management, they made up for in intelligence and work ethic. Nine of the ten teachers were white. They had one black teacher on the TPP staff. No New Orleanians managed to stay on the Prep faculty for more than six months. Crescent City Prep Principal Brian Rice had a Harvard MBA and was lured by the call of service after Hurricane Katrina. He left Wall Street to start a charter school. Completely familiar with the mecca of capitalism, Rice believed in its tenets. He preached competition, bottom lines, portfolios, turnaround and takeover. He openly said how the storm was a blessing, and the city had an opportunity to "wipe the slate clean." Rice openly blamed the union and former teachers for ruining public education in the city.

Rice wanted a different type of teacher.

"The quickest, most efficient way to turn around a failing school is to exchange the human capital."

He aggressively sought a partner who would provide those services. The state signed a contract with TPP for teachers, which scoured the market for young, smart talent. Rice also contracted with TTP, which charged an administrative fee, to replace many of the teachers he had originally hired for Prep—like Mr. Simon. As advertised, TPPers worked as if they were on a religious mission. They proved to be the types of workers that captains of industry and unions recruit. These primarily white young adults crafted lesson plans, tutored and organized day and night.

After his brief tenure at Prep, Mr. Simon could not stomach Rice, and was not particularly fond of the TPP hires, either. He saw the young teachers as contributing to the friction at the Prep/Johnson site. While the TPP teachers taught with a total command of their subject areas, their lack of experience resulted in poor classroom management. Prep and Johnson students regularly squabbled between classes. These problems often led Rice to expel numerous Prep students. Dr. Sarnacola, Mr. McClain and Mr. Simon lobbied vigorously to kick Crescent City Prep out of the Joseph Rainey building.

Once Rice got word of the proposed coup, he informed his teachers of the leadership's efforts. Soon thereafter Prep students openly threatened Johnson students. Subsequently, the different student bodies scrapped off campus regularly. The students seemed to play out the unresolved conflicts of the adults in charge of them.

When Mr. Simon dropped off the debate team, most went to their lockers before heading to waiting parents. Simon escorted those taking city buses. This particular time, he wanted to see the "ghosts."

Just as Loren and Katura claimed, the TPPers wandered

upstairs. They walked between their classrooms consulting with each other like it was 7:15 a.m. Monday. Mr. Simon noticed the racial makeup was as Katura described. Most of his colleagues would never work those hours. He thought to himself that black kids needed to see black teachers working the same hours as a team. Simon worried that Crescent City students would associate work hours with work ethic. Simon was impressed, but this was the same school that fired him. None of the teachers he worked with remained at the school.

Mr. Simon cautiously announced his presence when he stepped on their floor.

"Hello? It's me, Mr. Simon."

A group of the young professionals leaned out classrooms to see who was there. Several teachers recognized Simon's face but were unclear why he was there.

He approached one and asked, "Long night?"

The bright-eyed twenty-something, Katie said, "We're getting ready for Monday."

Mr. Simon said, "Wow. You should be down in the Marigny having fun."

Katie said, "We will. We're just finishing up."

"I'm Mr. Simon. I work at Johnson."

"I've seen you." Loren and Katura peeked down the hall. It was their first time in that section of the building.

Katie continued, "What are you doing up here?"

"Some Johnson students and I just got back from a debate tournament."

"How did you do?"

"Our team didn't do well, but our captain, Katura, took individual honors."

"Sounds great." Katie asked, "You worked at Prep at the

remote location?"

"Yes. It didn't last long. I didn't like the way the kids were handled."

"Yeah, we talk about that, too. It's a little militaristic at times."

Surprised to hear her agreement, Mr. Simon said, "Absolutely. How do you deal with it?"

"I don't agree with it, but students need structure. I'm willing to give it a try."

"The difference is Rice is willing to let you try."

At that point, Katura yelled down the hall that her parents would take the remaining students home.

"That's Katura, isn't it?"

"How did you know?

"I see her studying in the halls and library after school. She's adorable."

"Smart and dedicated. A lot like you, young lady. Where are you from?" Mr. Simon asked.

"Kansas City, but I moved from Baltimore."

"Johns Hopkins?

"How did you know?"

"Lucky guess."

"You're from New Orleans."

"Yes, I am. How did you know?"

"Lucky Guess."

"Why New Orleans?"

"After seeing what happened after Katrina I wanted to help. My professors had us study the educational system in the city. My Municipal Politics course took a trip to New Orleans as part of an alternative spring break my senior year. I fell in love with the place. I majored in political science and planned to go to law school after graduation, but I always wanted to teach. I thought if I joined TPP, I could do some good and live a bit of a dream."

"Did you ever think of working in Baltimore?"

"Why?"

"Baltimore city schools are just as bad. Its city government is in shambles. You could have helped there just as well."

"There is a real chance to change things in New Orleans."

"Chances exist everywhere."

"I disagree. If there is a silver lining to a tragedy, New Orleans is seeing one in its charter schools."

"Firing 7500 teachers is not my idea of a silver lining."

"The kids live in a cycle of poverty that only a good education can reverse. If we don't do what we can, we'll see the same things happen after another Katrina."

"I agree, but wasn't it true that unemployment also contributed to people being stranded outside the Superdome? How is firing locals and hiring people who won't stay long going to change anything in the long run? Don't we need consistency over time?"

"The world is watching us. If we succeed in New Orleans, America can have a new model to work from. Then I might go back to Baltimore or Kansas City, or even stay in New Orleans."

The conversation engaged Mr. Simon and Katie so deeply that they didn't notice the other teachers had wrapped up and were waiting for them.

One of the men said, "Y'all can finish the conversation over a beer."

Mr. Simon said, "Next time."

First Kiss

Once a semester, Mr. Simon and I invited local male dignitaries and a group of Johnson students to Chill's Barbershop, in Carrollton, as part of a tie-tying ceremony. The men purchased ties as gifts to young men we mentored. We included a popular salesman from a menswear store to give tie-tying lessons. In addition to neckwear, the men also treated the teens to haircuts and dinner. A jazz trio played as mentors and protégées discussed everything from career ideas to sex.

None of the boys and few of the men knew how to properly knot a bow-tie or make a double Windsor. Clip-on bow- and straight ties were an innovation that removed another intrinsic step in male bonding. Teaching how to properly tie ties and distinguish these knots has long been a rite of passage for manhood.

For this particular ceremony, I paired myself with Loren. Loren told Mr. Simon that he was excited about learning how to knot a bow-tie because the National Student Leadership Institute invited him and Katura to its annual conference, which was held in New Orleans. The conference included the Youth Leadership Gala, a formal, black-tie event. Formals and balls in New Orleans provide ample venues to show off fancy tie knots. But because of his family background, Loren did not have the familial and/or social links that introduced young men to traditional Mardi Gras balls, debutante balls or other events that required formal attire. Most of the men at the tie-tying ceremony were ensconced in the pomp and circumstance of New Orleans' social scene.

As soon as I presented Loren's fleur de lis patterned bow-tie, we discussed school work and running while practicing the knot. Like the rest of the boys, Loren was fully engaged in the lesson. There's a physical closeness that's required when teaching someone to tie. The teacher and student have to make themselves vulnerable, which is almost anti-masculine among urban youth culture. Hands have to be near and around another man's neck in a gentle way. This is allowed in a barbershop. It is one of the few places that allow closeness and positive intimacy between men and boys. In those moments and spaces, more open conversations occur.

While looking in the mirror, practicing tying his tie, Loren asked, "When is the right time to kiss a girl?"

I paused. I had to force myself to remove Katura from the question.

I replied, "I think, whenever you get into a physical relationship you have to have a higher level of commitment with that person."

"What do you mean? I'm not trying to marry anybody," he snapped.

"I mean, if you're committed to caring for that person's feelings, then a kiss is a natural thing."

Loren asked, "When was your first kiss? How old were you?"

"Wow!" I said, pausing to think back. "I think I was in eighth grade. I was in a park swimming pool. We saw each other in the pool every day. I knew she thought I was cute. I thought she was all right. Maybe she was just curious and didn't think I was really cute.

"To be honest, she had one of the best bodies I could imagine at the time."

"How did you make your move?"

"One day we were wrestling in the pool and we ended up hugging. We looked at each other nose to nose and started kissing."

Loren thought about it and asked, "Were you committed to her?"

"Well, I was committed to kissing her."

Loren let out a small laugh and said, "That sounds crazy."

"Yeah it does, but it's the truth. I wanted to learn how to kiss and touch a girl, and a swimming pool was a good setting. But I didn't want to just use her, either. It felt good that someone was attracted enough to want to kiss me."

"What happened after that?"

"I went to that pool every day from open to close, sun up to sun down."

Loren started laughing and said, "I bet your skin tanned black as night."

I continued, "We saw each other on occasion. I became so disappointed when she didn't show up. When she did come to the pool, we kissed at the end of the day. I think I was at her house once. Then one day near the end of summer, a group of boys from that neighborhood beat me up pretty bad. I was sore for weeks. I think it was because I was kissing one of 'their' girls."

"Did you go back?"

"No, never again."

"Did you see the girl again?"

"No, but I did learn how to kiss."

Loren smiled as if to say it was worth it.

"Do you remember her name?"

"Nope."

"What was all that talk about commitment?

I chuckled, realizing I'd talked the talk, but hadn't walked the walk.

"So, you're thinking about kissing Katura?"

"Yeah."

"Have you even held her hand yet?"

Loren said, "Kind of."

"If you can't hold her hand, then how're you going to jump into kissing?"

"That's why I'm talking to you!"

"You might want to start with her hand. Don't be afraid. When you know when and how to hold someone's hand, a kiss will be the next step."

"OK, Dr. Boyd."

"Thanks." Loren and I traded turns tying each other's bow-ties. After seven tries, he had it down. We discussed wearing a bow-tie at the upcoming gala, colognes, and moved on to haircuts.

* * *

All week Loren mulled over the conversation he had with Dr. Boyd. He made up his mind to hold Katura's hand in order to kiss her. On the Wednesday before the big biology exam, Loren insisted they study in the library. Katura typically called the study sessions, but because the test determined 30 percent of their grade, she didn't consider any ulterior motives.

As usual, Loren and Katura could stay as long as Mr. Simon

was in the building. Three-and-a-half hours passed since school closed. Ms. Garner shut down her library computer and bid Loren and Katura good evening.

Ms. Garner asked, "Studying for Ms. Loche's bio exam, are you?"

Katura said, "Yes ma'am."

"You two will do fine. I am so proud of you."

Growing impatient, Loren said, "Would you like me to walk you to your car?"

"You're so sweet. But Mr. Mike is still here, and I saw Mr. Simon's car."

As soon as the door shut, Loren asked, "Do you think they have copies of old biology books in here?"

"Probably. Why?"

"Ms. Loche always asks questions we didn't study in class. I bet she uses another book."

Katura excitedly said, "She probably does. Let's look in the library catalogue."

Loren and Katura tried to use the computer, but it required a password the now absent librarian had. They then went to the old card catalogue, which was still maintained. Ms. Garner did not want to let go of the hard copies of the Dewey Decimal System and taught every child how to use both. The computer system was off-line for maintenance and down enough, there was still sense to her approach.

As Katura searched, Loren watched her brown fingers pluck through the cards.

Before he could make his move, she said, "Found it."

It momentarily shook Loren's plans and confidence.

She continued, "They're in the special collections section near the media room."

Katura wrote down the numbers and started her march to the textbooks.

"Slow down," Loren said.

"Why?"

"You need to take your time. You may miss something."

At that moment, Loren reached for her hand and said, "Let's go together."

Shocked, Katura stopped as Loren started to move. It was if he tried to drag a stalled car. However, she did not let go.

He said, "What? I thought we were getting a biology book."

Katura's smile widened and the pair took their first steps hand in hand. Their pace slowed as they almost forgot where they were going. They continued to hold hands through the narrow aisles of books that ended in the corner of the library. As they approached the textbooks, they noticed movement in the dimly lit media room. They tried to make out who was in the room with the lights out. They backed into the aisle so they couldn't be seen.

As a couple moved closer to the glass in a tight embrace, Katura and Loren's eyes widened, and they whispered simultaneously, "Mr. Simon!"

They both whispered, "A Prep teacher. A white woman!"

After gawking at the couple making out, they eased back into the aisle.

Katura said, "That's the one he was talking to when we got back from the debate meet."

"You sure?"

"She's always here. I see her when you're running."

"Wait till Clarence hears."

"No. Clarence will spread it all over school. You'll get Mr. Simon in trouble, and we'll never be allowed to stay in the library again."

She looked into Loren's eyes and said, "You promise me that you'll never say anything."

He paused to think about the consequences of telling Clarence. He looked away for a moment then leaned near Katura and kissed her. The two slowly kissed as they held hands in the non-fiction section. The kiss removed all memory of Mr. Simon and Katie.

After the long-awaited kiss, Loren looked at Katura and said, "I promise."

Don't Get Caught with Your Pants Down

New Orleans public schools banded together to form a new cross-country league comprised of traditional and charter schools. The running program in general started to take root the previous spring semester after the initial track and field season proved successful. Coach D. developed a talented core of Johnson harriers who promised victory in the upcoming cross-country season. Not to be outdone, Crescent City Prep also developed a quality team. Several athletes who attended schools that barely kept their enrollments up flocked to charter schools citywide. Johnson and Prep attracted many hopefuls for track and field and cross-country.

Loren's running reflected his work ethic and rising confidence. In the first meet of the year, he placed fifth overall at a Catholic league invitational at City Park. After the first mile of his first race, Coach D. knew he had a winner. He began the year as the team's No. 1 runner.

Prior to the start of the race, Loren asked Coach D., "How should I go out?"

Coach D. replied, "Don't lose sight of the lead runner. Never lose sight."

After a slow start, Loren crept within a few feet of the lead runner and focused on the back of his jersey. With his eyes lasered to the back of that shirt, Loren chased one of the best runners in the city. He kept his pace until competitors out-kicked him in the final hundred meters. Loren didn't have the explosive speed for a sprint, but he had stamina for the long run.

The first three races were invitationals where only seven athletes competed. Clarence, who made the squad, didn't race until the first open meet of the season against marginal charter school competitors. The meet took place at Audubon Park on a cool but humid Saturday. This end-of-September weather gave the runners a little relief as they had expected to face sweltering heat.

When the bus arrived at the course, Coach D. directed Loren to lead the warm-up. The team began its warm-up jog along the five-kilometer course. Loren enjoyed his leadership position. He led the warm-up run and stretching drills with Clarence by his side.

This being Clarence's first race, Loren felt it his duty to help him through the start. Loren gave Clarence little nuggets of advice every five minutes as if he were a little brother.

Almost arrogantly, Loren said, "You may want to start out slow. You don't want to lead the pack. It's your first race."

Clarence asked, "How did *you* start your first race?"

"Coach D. told me to focus on the back of the lead runner's jersey."

"To win you have to look beyond the lead runner."

Loren replied, "All right now. You better follow through."

As they continued to prepare for the race, Loren asked Clarence, "Are you nervous?"

"Man. This is just cross-country. I've played football. Let's face it. It's a walk in the park," he said, laughing.

"OK," Loren said sarcastically, rolling his eyes at the lame joke.

Finally, Loren said to the team, "Game on. Take off the sweats."

The group disrobed and piled their clothes behind their starting box. The boys then did warm-up sprints from the starting line.

As Clarence made his way up to Loren after a hundred-meter burst, Loren noticed that Clarence wasn't wearing shorts. Confused, Clarence didn't get what he thought was a joke. The other athletes laughed loudly.

Loren asked, "What are you doing? You look crazy."

Clarence asked, "What?"

"You're in your underwear!"

Clarence looked down and saw his jersey was tucked into white briefs. Clarence said, "Oh, shit! I think I peeled them off when I yanked off my sweats."

Clarence sprinted away to look for his pants.

While the rest of the team laughed, Loren told them, "Keep doing your sprints."

Loren sprinted to Clarence to make sure he was dressed for the event, and said, "You're not nervous, huh?"

Clarence smirked and said, "I'm just showing the ladies what they came to see."

"Well, if we don't get to the start, the ladies are going to see us lose."

But at the sound of the gun, Johnson showed a competitive edge over the charter school teams. Johnson had out-practiced the other schools during the summer. Ten of the top fourteen runners hailed from Johnson. To Coach D.'s surprise, Clarence came in No. 3. As expected, Loren won with a commanding lead, but Clarence held up his end of the challenge. For most of the race Clarence used Loren's jersey as his follow-the-leader strategy.

Shocked at how fast Clarence had run, Loren asked him, "Man, how did you do it?"

Clarence said, "They say don't get caught with your pants down."

Pain

I didn't sleep the night before the state released the first official public school test scores in the fall of our second year. Just understanding the consequences of how individual schools are perceived is enough to induce insomnia for the most hardened school leader. I already knew what my individual school scores were, but how newspapers rank them influences funding, job security and reputation— all of which are vitally important to school survival. So I lay on my couch looking at music videos at 3:22 a.m. waiting to hear the slap of the paper on my doorstep.

Not yet two years after the storm, the rug could be pulled from under all my promises of "dramatic improvements" and "radical change" championed on television and radio interviews, at public forums, meetings with potential funders and in discussions with my board members and everyone else. School to school comparisons would be the measuring stick of success. My mother always told me not to worry about what other people thought. However, negative rankings could make the most confident person insecure. Poring over the possibilities in the middle of the night didn't help. I questioned whether my behaviors had changed since the paper kept the tally. Would we teach differently? Would we discipline students the same if there might be an investigative reporter at the school's main office? Would my blood pressure be lower if the paper wasn't aimed at my doorstep?

I taught in my public relations course at the university that good PR requires a cooperative relationship with the media, but their lust for controversy and failure made it difficult to be bedfellows. I had great relationships with individual reporters, but newspapers push alarmist tales over realistic nuance. The newspaper and the state didn't care that my 9th- through 12th-grade high school was different from the high school down the street: We were both judged by the same exam. It didn't matter how many students new to the city we accepted mid-year: We were judged on the same basis. Mentioning differences in our special needs populations, percent of free and reduced lunch students, parental educational levels and number of students expelled were heard as excuses. The state held all schools to the same acid test, so we were the same. This type of illogic compounded my restlessness.

As I lay across my couch awaiting the newspaper, I visualized two scenarios. The first was being ranked in the top quartile. I imagined follow-up interviews, disingenuously saying in my best professorial voice, "Test scores are not the reason why we exist. If they represent anything, test scores are evidence of the daily hard work of faculty, staff and students." The second scenario was what I would say if the school hit the bottom quartile. "We don't teach tests; we teach for the future." I manufactured spin like a washing machine. I knew what I was getting into when I took the job. I just hadn't realized it would be so painful. Superintendents, CEOs and principals are paid to take pot shots.

At my schools, if we ranked poorly, the university faculty would ask, "Why aren't you like Prep?" I had to face the state board of education with the seminal question: Why aren't your schools more successful? Operational staff would use performance to rate my abilities. However, the most pain comes from knowing that low scores generally mean kids probably are not learning. Not giving them a chance at a better life eclipsed any of my failures.

* * *

When the paper arrived, I rushed clumsily to the door. I could see the word "schools" above the fold. The headline read, "Charter schools outpace rest of state." The headline gave me some solace. However, I wanted to see how we fared against our competitors.

Inside the news section, rankings were placed prominently in the center of the page. With my index finger I counted my schools' positions from the top. I started with the high schools. Prep was in the first quartile. I became slightly depressed. However, Johnson soon followed. Three points and two schools separated them. They both ranked in the top quartile. All my elementary schools were above the 50th percentile. Not good, but not horrible. All four were "passing" according to state standards. After reading the article three times and performing an eyeball analysis, I hit the sack again.

I thought about the spin cycle: "We are better than we were, but we have work to do." That would buy me another year to conjure more magic.

Fourth Fridays

The fourth Friday of every month eventually became a popular and productive assembly for Loren's class. When it began, Loren invited his cabinet so they could establish a calendar of events for the month. The group met in Mr. Simon's room. Loren and Katura invited various school clubs to work out calendar details. Two groups became four; four became eight. Eventually the meeting was attracting attention from teachers and administrators. The administration asked the group to move into the upper classmen's gym/cafeteria/assembly hall. Most extracurricular activities were constructed, developed and promoted at the meetings. More than three-quarters of the 10th grade came to "Fourth Friday" gatherings.

The old gym's entrance opened under the basketball hoop opposite a dark, cherry-brown wooden, stage. The gym was on the third floor and hadn't been flooded. The school colors— red, white, and blue— regaled visitors as they entered the auditorium. The smell of sweaty young men, women and lacquer created a distinctive scent. The aroma combined mystique and nostalgia like a grandmother's attic. Older, white alumni pressured the district to restore and maintain the facility. The decision to expand the cafeteria into the gym brought a great deal of heat on board members. Alums did not want their precious gym ruined by a food court. A compromise was made to appease the older alums. The deal meant the school had to hire new maintenance workers to clean the space. The gym's spotless yet old-fashioned look gave the space a feel of a historic preservation site.

Despite its placement, students never walked on the school mascot painted on the floor at center court. The eagle was so revered that the annual retracing of the mascot closed the cafeteria and served as part of homecoming celebration. It was one of the few highlights of the school year; yet, the alums could have managed to donate matching lunch furniture, students and administrators thought. Bright, outdated turquoise lunch tables clashed with the room's somber decor. However, on one historic Fourth Friday, the setting provided a fitting milieu for one of Loren's most significant legacies.

With the exception of lunch tables, administrators guarded every aspect of the old gym. The principal, Dr. Sarnacola, assigned teachers to monitor the meetings. Loren paid close attention to the rotation of teachers. He suspected Mr. McClain's distrust of the students. Loren made careful notes of the teachers assigned. Eventually, Loren predicted what teachers would come. He also observed how they interacted with students. Some helped by opening doors or providing office supplies and advice. Most teachers simply checked in once or twice, then returned to their rooms to grade homework and tests. The rookie teachers assigned to watch students on Friday kept themselves busy by flirting with each other in the teachers' lounge downstairs. After a few months of trust-building and monitoring, teachers were less watchful.

Fourth Fridays produced swift and decisive consensus on a myriad of issues ranging from club elections, event dates, requests for funding, how funding was spent and information disseminated. Clubs and organizations presented their plans with other interested student organizations. It was a place where the gospel choir discussed concert plans with the jazz ensemble. Unusual alliances formed. Students from the chess club consulted with the pep squad. A representative cross-section of Johnson came to meet, greet, build and network.

The students also socialized. Dr. Sarnacola allowed free dress on Fridays, and students sported stylish casual wear. Fourth Fridays became the closest thing to a 10th-grade happy hour. Girls clambered for Loren's attention. Boys ogled girls' tight jeans. Katura stood by Loren's side as they conducted business and kept close watch on his eyes.

As their 10th-grade year progressed, the discussions matured along with the students. Teacher supervision waned while gatherings became more student structured. Although the Fourth Friday group grew, the conclave maintained an intimacy. Discussions of Fourth Friday affairs rarely reached the ears of faculty or administrators. Students learned they could plan huge events and avoid their awareness. Given their distant proximity to faculty, hiding information from teachers wasn't difficult.

The students tested clandestine operations by throwing birthday parties for some of the school's favorite teachers. Loren's executive team was amused at how easily they could set up such a large space and plan intricate details for events. Loren liked the secrecy so much that the group even threw parties for unpopular teachers like Ms. Eberthal. For Ms. Eberthal's birthday, they invited forty-five relatives to the party. This was an amazing feat. Not only did they secretly gather family information, but students also used school resources to make calls, mailings, and hire entertainment. Loren laughed at her surprise that relatives from all over the city appeared at Johnson High School. Ms. Eberthal's birthday signified that students had untapped power. The success and completion of "Project Eberthal" signified their readiness for something bigger.

November's Fourth Friday was a major benchmark. That meeting was the last before two major standardized tests the third week of December. Tenth grade was the first opportunity to take the Graduate Exit Examination and the ACT. It was a year of good work and effort since Loren's presidency, and Dr. Boyd, Dr. Sarnacola and Mr. Simon all wanted validation of their efforts through these tests. The tests also occurred two days after the city cross-country championships. Johnson students' futures rested heavily on the state exam and the cross-country championships. But students felt confident and ready.

Loren's earlier pledge was about to be tested. He hadn't mentioned anything about not taking the state exam since he overheard Mr. McClain argue with Mr. Simon a year earlier. Even though Katura was the only person to hear Loren's pledge, he repeated it a hundred times in his sleep.

"I will not take another standardized test."

But so much of Loren's future hinged upon a passing grade on the test. He had a perfect record on his transcript. He successfully completed and excelled in the highest levels of math and science courses offered at Johnson. Teachers, coaches, student and community members saw Loren as a model student. With Katura's help, Loren became the most disciplined, hard working, and proud student in school.

Since he was elected into office, the once maligned 9th-grade class had started to excel. It was undeniable that a child could do what teachers, parents, money, and policymakers could not—inspire. His class was perceived differently from preceding classes.

Among 10th-graders, there wasn't a real distinction between honors students and the general education track. In fact, many of the privileges honors kids received were expanded to include the entire class. Enrollment in special education classes dropped more than 75 percent. Dozens of students seemed to miraculously lose their emotional disturbance and attention deficit disorders. Suspensions plummeted. Tenth-grade attendance was near perfect. Not only were 10th- and now 9th-graders twice as likely to be in school, they were more likely to fully participate in the classroom. Honor roll membership doubled and tripled. Student and teacher morale rose to all-time highs. It was Loren who inspired and lead the students to these achievements, though the students did the good work.

At the November Fourth Friday, Loren and Katura sat at the far end of an eight-foot table on the right side of the podium. They shared whispers and laughs as various groups spoke. After several ceremonial functions and honors to individuals and clubs, the sergeant-at-arms called Loren to the stage for a few closing words. Typically, Loren spoke last. He delivered succinct, pointed speeches. As soon as his name was called, the crowd clapped and shouted his name— as churchgoers might midway through a sermon. They shouted, "Mr. Pres."

He walked slowly toward the podium contemplating exactly what he was going to say. Loren knew the content of his speech, but wasn't sure if he should say it. He looked at friends for a few moments as his audience settled.

"Over the last year, our wonderful class has made remarkable strides. We've sidestepped all the teachers' old opinions and stereotypes. You may not know this, but we're doing things no one expected us to accomplish. Johnson High School's 'Class of Respect' is making it happen."

The crowd applauded and formed the "X" sign.

Loren's tone deepened, and a seriousness fell over him.

"We've been seeking respect and achievement. We've been trying to get teachers to see we can learn. Our class proved we did not have to learn on opposite sides of the school. Teachers taught us how 'separate but equal' didn't work in the past. Then why should it work now?"

The crowd's applause rose again, and Loren paused to receive it.

"We learn together."

The students gave Loren a standing ovation.

"We've been searching for respect for a while, and we still can't get it. Despite our attendance records, grades, community service, and more, we still can't get respect. Sure, they give us a smile and a pat on the back. You hear them say, 'Good job. I'm so proud of you.' I don't know about you, but I'm beyond gold stars like they gave in kindergarten."

Everyone chuckled.

"We've mastered their theories and their history. We use proper English and perform on athletic fields and in concert halls. We play their games and sing their songs. We do everything we are asked to do at the highest levels. Without doubt, Johnson's class of respect is the best class in the entire state. So, if we know how good we are, and they know how good we are, why do we have to prove it again on a state examination?"

The crowd's stares suggested Loren needed to explain himself. Loren pulled out a sheet of paper.

"The third week of December, we are supposed to take the Graduate Exit Exam and the ACT in order to 'indicate what students should know and be able to do as a result of their educational experiences,'" Loren read directly from the state document.

"If anyone of us is unable to achieve 'sufficient proficiency levels,' then we will be held back from advancing to our junior year and timely graduation," Loren said sarcastically.

"Sure, they help you by forcing you to take an 'individualized summer session' that supposedly will help you reach sufficient educational levels, but that's not good enough for me. Let's get this straight. I will use myself as an example. I have a straight-A average here at Johnson. I have taken every upper-level course offered. After all those 'indicators of success,' the state is telling me that I may not graduate if I don't pass *an additional* test."

There was a rustle in the audience that suggested discomfort. Some were not sure where Loren was headed. Others suddenly realized the state exam's power.

"They just assumed we would take the test and everything would be fine. They never asked the question, 'What if we don't take it?'"

Many in the audience considered the purpose of the state exam for the first time. Loren allowed the crowd to rumble for a few moments, and then he continued.

"I often ask myself, 'Why haven't I found respect?' After accomplishing almost every goal a student can, I've found out why. I haven't found respect because I've looked in the wrong places. We can't and won't find respect from teachers, administrators, coaches or parents. They tell us we are mere children, incapable of making important decisions or accepting serious responsibility. No, we can't find respect in schools. So where do we find respect?"

Loren continued.

"I found respect in me— self-respect."

The crowd let out even, strong applause. After the response,

Loren moved on.

"I've found it in you and me. We believe in ourselves like no one else, and we must act on our beliefs. We must show this school, city, and state that we respect ourselves and are able to make decisions that positively affect our lives.

"We can decide because we have knowledge, self-respect and power. Have you noticed how much attention this school receives because of our hard work? Newspapers, television, and radio reporters regularly seek us out to discuss how exceptional we are. The administration brags at their conferences about how *they* turned this school around. As they talk out of the sides of their mouths, we hold our tongues because we know the real attitudes of the teachers. I remember how teachers threatened to call Child Protective Services on me because they said I came to school dirty. My hair is still nappy, and my shoes are just as worn, but they're not calling CPS now."

The crowd chuckled again.

"I'm the ambassador for 'at-risk youth' instead of a menace to society. All we have to do is snap our fingers toward the media, and they come running. All we have to do is blink, and all those awards that these administrators received will fall off the shelves. I just interviewed with Channel 9 last week. They would jump out of their shoes to break the story that there may be trouble in paradise. Too bad people don't recognize that we know what our class means to this school district. Something tells me that I need to exercise my power and self-respect and let somebody know."

A mixture of laughter and applause filled the air. Loren knew he was winning over the crowd. His excitement removed the last bit of apprehension from his voice. He'd waited a year for this moment and was not about to waste it.

"I'm about to do something with my self-respect. I've been meaning to tell, but I wanted to make sure you were ready. Remember when we took the first version of the state examination last year? They didn't count. None of us were held back. If they did, I would have been held back because I marked the letter 'A' for every single problem. I wrote a little note on the exam. It read, 'These are the letters you will see on every report card.'"

The crowd looked around in amazement. Smiles of disbelief slid across faces. Loren let the crowd absorb what he said then pushed his agenda.

"After a long, boring, and drawn-out argument with Mr. McClain and some lazy counselors, I made a promise. I told them I would never take a standardized test again. Many of the teachers and administrators who heard my promise forgot it. I cannot and will not take the GEE or ACT."

The crowd looked perplexed and fell deadly silent. But they realized what he was asking. All his peers assumed they would pass the GEE, get great marks on the ACT, graduate high school and go to college. Their path was assured. The students also assumed that standardized tests were the means to their goals. Most thought Loren was committing educational suicide. They had come so far. No one had expected their success. They challenged assumptions every day. Johnson High School owed Loren the sophomore class's success. That is why they stood in silence. Every decision he made had proved correct. The students trusted Loren more than their parents or teachers. Loren gave most of them a glimpse of their futures.

"I am not taking the GEE or ACT in the next few days, and I want you all to do the same."

The crowd gasped.

Loren continued, "We have gained so much in the last two

years. Why should these tests determine so much? Don't all the A's on my report card and yours tell our potential? Don't they trust our teachers' assessments? Why must we prove ourselves again and again?

Focused, Loren said, "What I've just said might scare you, but if you're confident, you won't be afraid. We must share the power we have with other students outside of our school. How can we do this? We walk away from the examinations, and ask our administration to back us and our hard work."

A student jumped to his feet and said, "Yo! What are you saying? I'm the first one in my family who might go to college."

Another said, "I've got to get out of New Orleans. You're not going to pay my tuition."

"We can't change a state with one protest. I want to go to college, and you're talking about holding me back from graduation."

Students' dissent rose to a rumble.

"Look, do our schools really believe in us? If it were not for a few teachers who wanted to change how our school taught us, we would not be in this position of strength. Yeah, there are a few teachers. But we have to show other students this system doesn't work."

A student yelled, "My mother will kill me!"

"What have your parents done?" Loren asked.

Caught off guard by Loren's audacity, the crowd gasped again.

He continued, "I'm serious. The only time parents come to school is to bring us back from suspensions. Sure they love us, but they can't help us. None of them are on the school board. The PTA is an empty house. They can't help us with homework. We've passed most of our parents academically already. Mr. Simon fills out our summer job paperwork because they can't help us. We are what our community has to offer. And our community does nothing but hurt us. I am tired of police thinking that every black face belongs to a gang member. I'm tired of preachers and drug dealers being the only black folks driving fancy cars. I'm tired of white folks locking their car doors at stoplights when they see us.

"We can't give credit to our school, parents, or community. *We* made the difference in this school."

The crowd slowly started cheering and clapping.

Taking advantage of the momentum, Loren said, "Now is the time we let other students across the state know they also can change the educational system."

At this point the students hung on his every word.

"I'm not going to let these test-makers erase my year of hard work. Are you?"

Scattered audience members yelled, "No!"

"Before this class started it, Johnson didn't have a school debate team. They didn't have a chess club. Before us, the administration separated 'honors' students from general education, and those few privileged students represented Johnson for everything. Let me remind you we demanded we join these honors programs. We demanded that we compete. Once "general education" kids started to win competitions and represent the school at the highest levels, then Johnson was forced to tear down the walls between honors, general education and even special education sections of the school.

"We did this. It's just not fair that our hard work is judged through two tests that can't possibly measure all we've accomplished. It's time to send a message to the system that these tests do nothing but keep people like us down.

"I have prepared myself to refuse both exams, and I understand if you don't follow my lead. However, remember these tests keep us out of the best colleges in the state. In the past Johnson had some of the lowest scores in the state. If our scores were low, whose fault was it? You think not having frogs to dissect had anything to do with not doing well on the science portion of the test? What about test tubes? What about science teachers instead of substitutes? Oh, I forgot. What about textbooks in the beginning of the year? Did our scores motivate old teachers to work harder or new teachers to stay? We've done everything we can at Johnson. Who should be punished for low scores?

"I'm ready to use my power against this oppression, and make a public announcement on Monday that I am not taking the exams. If our entire class walks out, we let the state and our peers know we will not be pushed around."

One student stood up after a pause and asked, "What if they fail us? What then?"

Loren said, "I assure you that we will go on to the 11th and 12th grades and graduate. The district has put too much in our class. They need us."

Another student yelled, "I read that Roosevelt High School is planning to hold back 50 percent of their students. What makes you so sure that they won't hold us back?"

Loren replied sharply, "We cannot be compared to any school in the district. The only news that Roosevelt makes is bad news. We are the chosen ones, and we must save schools like Roosevelt from themselves."

A girl in the back said, "You keep talking about media. How are we going to get them involved?"

"After Channel 9 interviewed a group of us last week, I let the reporter know about our test day plans. She gave me a card and told me to call her first. I did not tell her that I gave other media people the same information, and they all gave me cards. If you don't want to participate, go to school on Monday, take the test, and be happy.

"Early Monday morning, I'll call the news and tell them our class refuses to take the mandatory state exam. When significant numbers of reporters arrive, I will read a brief statement explaining why we chose not to take the test."

Another voice asked, "Explain to me why we are protesting the ACT now?"

Loren stated, "Most of us have not taken the ACT yet. We need to send a message to all the test takers in the state and the admissions offices at the state universities about our not taking the test."

Loren continued, "I need some of you to make signs and spread the word to students who aren't here. This is top-secret. We have to take everyone by surprise. No slip-ups to parents, brothers, sisters, friends, dogs, or cats. Only our class knows. If this is too much for you, take the exam."

Loren paused and murmurs resonated through the gym. People were stirring, and Loren took a deep breath. He looked relieved as if he had reached his goal.

After a few minutes, Loren broke the silence.

"Listen. You do not have to decide today. Think about it this weekend. Come to the cross-country championship tomorrow to see how serious I am. If you are down for the cause, so be it. If you want to take the test, so be it, too. Remember, this is Project Eberthal."

Loren then returned to his seat, turned to Katura and asked, "How did I do?"

She looked him in the eyes and shook her head in amazement.

Loren responded, "That good!"

After an exchange of smiles, Loren said, "Let's go."

Race Day

I decided to take a group of students, including Katura, to the championship meet at City Park. The red, white, and blue provided the only color on an otherwise gray, rainy day. The downpour obscured my vision through the windshield. It was no surprise that the entire community convened for this full-fledged rivalry despite the weather. Johnson devotees, Loren disciples, loyal teachers, parents and students, and a curious media eagerly awaited the drama. Though all present for different reasons, our hopes brought us to a crossroads. The line was drawn across surnames, friends and communities. Each group felt the meet was a symbolic validation.

The student-run Johnson Business Alliance sold red, white, and blue Jazz Fest ponchos as well as handkerchiefs and pom-poms throughout the week and at the venue. Johnson fans arrived wearing hoods and waving flags. From our view, spots of the opposing team's colors were sprinkled over the scene. Katura sat next to me, and I could almost hear her heart racing as we pulled up to the field. Katura wore Loren's training jacket, which came in handy because the unseasonably cool weather made the rain icy cold.

After searching for fifteen minutes, I squeezed into a parking space about five minutes' walk from the start. But I took an unusual amount of time to parallel park, and Katura's eyes rolled up in her head as I backed up a third time. Before I placed the truck in park, Katura jumped out and began a mad dash toward the starting line. The three other students in the truck waited patiently.

The rains had poured all night on the open fields, which were ravaged by the storm. My student passengers finally broke into a sprint for the starting line. Recalling my cross-country days, I tried to catch them. After a few strides, my shoes were soaked. My jacket's hood flapped in the air, and my locks dripped down my neck and onto my back. Finally at the start, I searched for the team and Loren. They typically waited along the park trails until the race started.

The crowd had lined the periphery of the course. A mix of fans, reporters, photographers, and spectators convened at the start and finish line. The swarm created a tunnel for the competitors to run through. Fans carried signs of support for all the team members. Surprisingly, you could still make out the dripping paint and markers on the signs. Signs honoring our hero's first school victory, *Loren for President,* were everywhere.

It was fifteen minutes before the starting gun, so I found my way toward the front. I felt the throng's excitement as I weaved through the crowd. Students also acknowledged Katura's bond with Loren.

One girl said affectionately, "Make way for the first lady," and Katura responded with a proud smile.

I finally exited the caverns of soggy poster board and thought to myself how every parent, teacher, and student seemed to have come out. As I nestled in a spot near the starting line, I noticed that the red, white, and blue group became less dense. A prominent contingent of a purple and stark gold filled Johnson's space. Our rivals were present in full force. The Crescent City Prep Bulldogs staked their claim past the starting line along the final 50 meters of the course.

As the rivals emerged onto the trail, their fans barked and howled, the Bulldog yell. Leading the pack was the school's best runner, sophomore Dirk Thompson. Because of injuries and schedule conflicts Johnson never raced the Bulldogs with Dirk in the lineup. However, his times on common courses let the team and coaches know he was a formidable opponent. While evenly matched among the top runners in the league, Prep's depth was much greater.

Dirk's machismo swagger was over the top. He wore a black fitted skullcap that covered his eyebrows. He postured like a rapper at an awards show. Girls from all the schools fawned over him. He stayed in front of his fellow teammates.

In the moments before the race, Dirk hollered down the starting line, "Whoooose House!"

The crowd replied with a raucous chorus of barks.

The Bulldogs' team did several warm-up runs. Dirk bellowed barks that echoed above all the cheers and signs as they exercised. Unlike his teammates, Dirk stripped down to his uniform in front of his fans. You could hear the crowd's boisterous applause and the girls' screams. After the outburst, Dirk initiated the school's traditional call and response. He signaled for a reply with a hand behind his ear.

He then asked, "Whoooose hoooouuuuse?"

The crowd responded, "Doooog's hoooouuuuse!"

"Whoooose Hoooouuuuse?"

"Doooog's Hoooouuuuse!"

The chant went on for a few rounds until Loren showed.

As soon as the red, white, and blue saw the Johnson Harriers, cheers exploded like cannons. Loren headed the group with Clarence on his right. Sincere adulation for this hometown hero inspired more outbursts. No prior student organized our community in any substantive direction. So we cheered wholeheartedly for him. Moreover, the applause was a response to Prep's cheers. The deafening sounds of the downpour, claps, barks, cowbells, and whistles were an appropriate prequel to this first cross-country championship. As the Johnson team approached their fans, individual cheers for Loren began.

"All right, Loren, do what you do best!"

"Show them who's president, Loren!"

"Walk those dogs, Loren!"

As usual, he seldom acknowledged the crowd. But his tightened jaw and blank stare prompted more cheers and applause. They knew he was focused.

Soon before Johnson's ovation died down, you could hear the Prep chant winding up. It started as a rumble, but ended as a roar.

"Whoooose Hooouuuse?"

"Dooooog's Hooooouuuuse!"

"Whoooose Hooouuuuse?"

"Dooooog's Hooooouuuuse!"

Dirk Thompson led the effort. When the chant became too much to bear, the Johnson faithful raised their voices. The noise was deafening. Both sides acted as if the other six schools present weren't competing.

* * *

In the moments before the race began a still fell over spectators and participants, and the rain subsided. The crowd looked up at the sky as the sun's rays peeked through clouds. Umbrellas slowly closed and hoods left heads. The verbal warfare that transpired before the race seemed like friendly whispers compared to visible tension emanating from the heads of those athletes. It was time to let the kids have their moment. Each team was positioned along the starting line in their designated area. Although the athletes had been running all year, their eyes told a story of inexperience and uncertainty. The two principles, Loren and Dirk, were completely still. Other athletes bounced around to keep themselves warm, their minds empty of the impending struggle.

Clarence was on bended knee stretching. He had a peculiar calm about him. It seemed as if he were elsewhere. It was hard for me to see, but it looked like he was talking to himself. His head bobbed as if in conversation, but his lips didn't move.

Then the starter moved to the microphone. The gray-haired starter had been a part of every cross-country championship since before the storm. The pure applause was an acknowledgement of his status. He uttered the regular spiel to the competitors.

"I have two commands, 'on your marks,' and when the gun sounds, 'go.'"

The runners dug their toes into the mushy soil. It was time. As quickly as the ovation rose, it fell to silence. The runners' eyes shot to the starter.

"On your marks!"

The gun banged and the crowd's yells followed. A mass of forty-two runners hustled clumsily down the grassy field. A few runners fell and were trampled by runners immediately behind. The chaotic first dash always produced casualties. The hourglass shape of the first section of the course favored individuals with prodigious opening speed. Dirk was famous for his incredible sprints, and he did not disappoint. He launched off the starting line like a rocket. After the first three steps he had a deep lead. It didn't take Dirk long to separate himself from the other runners. Loren was a weak starter. He had to work his way to the front.

Dirk's place was not surprising, but Clarence's was. Clarence was right beside Dirk as they entered the small opening in the woods. For a while the crowd mistook Clarence for Loren.

One father said with confidence, "Did you see Dirk and Loren take off? This race is going to be good."

I was sure who was who. However, Loren was in good position. He entered the woods sixth. After the first ten runners passed, I made my way toward the half-mile point. I knew the tangential paths that were free from spectators.

I ran as fast as I could to position myself. My careful strides were carried by thoughts of Loren. I had to get to the half-mile mark first.

After I jumped a huge rock, I was about 40 meters shy of the half-mile marker. Many others planted themselves about 50 meters up the trail. As soon as I hit the runner's trail, I heard the footsteps of the first runner coming around the bend. It was Clarence. Before I awoke from my astonishment, Clarence flew by. He had a sizable lead. I watched his back as he turned the corner ahead.

Dirk made his way around the bend. There was a look of certainty on his face. Surely Dirk thought the race was his. Where was Loren? Dirk then hurried around the bend toward Clarence.

Loren finally showed a distant third. While I was sure Loren could make up this deficit, he didn't seem to be running his usual smooth pace. His eyes were focused on the ground. He seemed to be running in a stupor. I screamed at the top of my lungs, "Come on, Pres! You can do it!" Loren's limp had returned. He sluggishly passed me. A host of Crescent and Johnson runners fighting for position were not far behind.

One Johnson runner yelled, "Pick it up, Loren! We're coming!"

As soon as the second group passed, I ran across the path so that I could make the mile mark. I closed my eyes for a moment and considered what was wrong.

I scurried to the mile marker. Was he sick? Did he twist an ankle? Someone must have stepped on his heel. It was probably a Bulldog who tripped him. Whatever happened it couldn't end like this.

I made my way up to the mile-marker where dozens of people camped before the start of the race. I overheard conversations.

One woman said, "I can't wait to see Loren. He is truly a blessing. Loren is going to be president one day. Just wait and see."

The gentleman beside me said, "Loren should be coming around the bend shortly."

All the talk was about Loren. I kept shaking my head. We hadn't considered Loren losing.

The crowd rushed behind me waiting to see where the runners were positioned at the mile point. Most people hadn't seen what I had. The *Loren for President* signs were up and waving assertively. The enthusiasm and anticipation were high. A red, white, and blue shadow peeked through the trees. The crowd's fervor mounted, and the horde began stirring. As Clarence emerged in first place at the mile marker, the buzz changed to bewilderment.

The crowd became still. Many people looked as if they did not recognize Clarence. People were whispering, and we forgot to support this new man.

At that point I belted out, "You're our man, Clarence! You're our man!"

We were so wrapped up in the "perfect president" we forgot to recognize leadership. Clarence's brilliant running radiated a new strength. He seemed at peace as he glided through the crowd and his face glowed. It seemed that he was at ease with himself. There was no pain or discomfort despite his furious pace.

I overheard a few fans ask if the No. 1 runner was the same Clarence from the neighborhood. Most kept wondering where Loren was. Johnson fans were dazed. A few pulled themselves together to cheer for Clarence. As everyone turned to see who was next to come round the bend, the purple and gold color clad Dirk came into view. Their gladiator resuscitated the barking from Prep fans.

His face looked hungry for a win. He strained to catch up with every step. You could see Clarence was the only person who threatened Dirk. Dirk furiously stormed by the uncontained crowd.

When Dirk exited the path, I started counting the seconds between him and Loren. "Twenty-four." Loren was still in contention. I exhaled a deep sigh. Then I thought, What's wrong? Among the shallow screams of praise, I searched to find something that could inspire. Then I saw Loren pass Katura at the mile marker.

I could hear her scream, "Will you have the will and courage to match your commitments?"

At that point color erupted into the scene. It was if he was running in his sleep, and someone threw cold water in his face. He shook his head as if he was trying to wake up from his sleep walk.

When Loren gritted his teeth it sparked something in the

crowd. At one point all I could see was a thousand hands pointing in Clarence's direction. The claps intensified with the level of sheer will on Loren's face. Feeding off the crowd, his energy soared and his stride became smoother. His pace quickened. He bounced off the puddles beneath his feet with each stride. After the first few moments past the opening mile, I sensed a change in his spirit. When Loren slipped into hidden spaces along the course, the crowd's volume dissipated, and I immediately charged to the finish.

* * *

The last half-mile of the race was visible to the spectators. Clarence exited the woods, followed by Dirk and Loren. All three showed labored gaits and were nearly exhausted. Clarence set too fast a pace for them to continue. You could see them all stumble from fatigue as they ran. The crowd erupted as parents, faculty and staff cheered joyfully for their athletes.

As Clarence, Loren, and Dirk came closer to the finish, the crowd lined the home stretch. The string of flags that hovered over the restrictions lay uselessly on the ground. The onlookers overtook a television reporter and cameraman. Officials fought the crowd back so the runners had a clear path. Police pushed people behind the artificial lines. I also pushed my way through to the front. I could finally see that Dirk, Clarence and Loren were shoulder to shoulder with 100 meters to go. I leaned over several Prep fans for a clearer view. I counted every step and every step counted. Despite the pushing and shoving, everyone was focused on the three athletes as they panted toward the finish.

With 50 meters left Clarence took a slight lead. His eyes were wide and his lips pressed tightly together. Loren and Dirk seemed stifled by Clarence's sudden position. Screams shot through the air like fireworks and Loren made a last effort. Eyes squinting shut, Loren left Dirk and stormed ahead. Dirk responded with his own burst. With every bit of energy, Loren passed Clarence and lunged to the tape. Both Loren and Clarence hit the ground and slid on the wet grass. Dirk crossed the line still standing. The small string wrapped around Loren's chest signified the victor.

Completely exhausted, both athletes lay in the puddles. Side by side with their faces to each other, Loren and Clarence hugged. Dirk reached for Loren's hand. After Loren climbed up, the two embraced and exchanged a few words. Dirk and Loren then hauled up Clarence. He could barely stand. The officials pushed Loren, Dirk and Clarence to the sidelines and wrapped them in towels as runners continued to pour across the finish. Fans, coaches and media did the rest of their jobs with the rest of the pack. But the victors had claimed their spoils.

Statement of Purpose

"Look, there's the principal. Jim, get your camera up the stairs. Come on! Is everything ready? Good.

"Angel Tyler, WBDC. Dr. Sarnacola, can we get a few words regarding the entire 10th grade refusing to take the General Exit Examination?"

"At this time, I don't have a comment. We are trying to control the situation out here," the principal said, sounding nervous.

The reporter told her cameraman, "Jim, make sure you get a shot of all the teachers looking out the doors and the windows. Let's grab a quick statement from that teacher over there."

"Angel Tyler, WBDC. Can we get a few words regarding the 10th-grade state competency examination walkout?"

"I'm not sure what's going on, but that can't be right."

"Can I get your name and position here at Johnson?"

"My name is Ms. Jones, and I am a math teacher here at Johnson."

"Ms. Jones, why do you think the sophomore class is refusing to take the examination?"

"I'm not sure why. Johnson's 10th grade is one of the best classes in the state. We take pride in everything we do at Johnson."

"Several of the students' picket signs read, 'End institutionalized oppression.' What do you think they mean, Ms. Jones?

"I'm not sure. I'm afraid I can't answer more questions."

The reporter turned to the cameraman and said, "Jim, let's get closer to the action."

Jim said, "This is the craziest. These kids are incredible. We just did a story about that Loren kid last week."

"He's the one that gave me the tip, but it looks like he did the same to every other station. Look at this circus. TV, radio, print. Next thing you know cable and Internet networks will be here. Jim, get a shot of that poster. Wow. 'No sellout, No test-taking.' Reminds me of my college days. Look! Let's get some mic time with that person standing in front of the doors.

"Angel Tyler, WBDC. Can we get a few words regarding the exam walkout?"

"They are committing academic suicide. I'm so embarrassed by their insolence and ignorance."

"Can I get your name and position here at Johnson?"

"Mr. McClain, English teacher and head of counseling."

"Mr. McClain, the 10th-grade class president, Loren Wise, has been quoted as saying, 'The neediest students are punished by the state examination,' and 'Teachers no longer teach children. They teach tests.' Is there any truth to his statements?"

"Loren is a boy who has received too much attention over the last year. I only wished that his talent exceeded his ego. There is absolutely no truth to his statements. True to form, Loren and his misguided ideas are cutting students' throats. I recommend that you ignore Loren Wise."

"What do you think spurred the protest?"

"Ignorance, arrogance, and fear. Sometimes the most successful students are afraid to take tests because they're the ones who are expected to do well. Everyone expects this class to thrive.

However, can the students handle the pressure of expectations? I calculate their side-stepping is a clear indication of their fear of success. In fact, Loren showed signs of this in my own class."

"How so?"

"When things got tough for Loren, he often sat speechless or confused."

"What do you think will be the result of their protest?"

"We have regulations and rules in this state. Every single person who is out waving their signs instead of #2 pencils won't be promoted."

The reporter turned her attention to the podium where students gathered. The crowd of students and reporters merged. Loren moved to the microphone.

Directing the crowd, Loren said, "Students! Students! Can I ask that everyone gather round the podium? Dr. Sarnacola, you don't have to encourage us to go back in school. It will be over in a few minutes. Students, I need calm. We are about to begin.

"I want to address our panicked parents, teachers and the press. First, I want to send a message to the state department of education, our local school district, and the university.

"My name is Loren Wise, and I am the sophomore class president and one of the organizers of this event. I want to thank all of the class for coming out, but I especially want to thank our Vice-President Katura Price for helping me coordinate this event."

A reporter yelled out, "Why is the 10th grade protesting the GEE?"

"Over the last two years, our class has improved tremendously in all academic areas. Some of the best students in the state attend Johnson. We owe our successes to a few good teachers who gave us the skills to think critically. The rest of the teachers did a great job in forcing us to learn the state exams. While we appreciate the work that went into teaching these tests, the 10th grade opposes the harm they cause to students. Teachers are focused on tests— not students."

Another reporter asked, "Isn't that the way the GEE is supposed to work? It seems that the teachers did their jobs."

"Teachers who taught subjects and not tests made the difference. Most kids in urban schools are not taught to think critically. They are taught to memorize a few questions for a test. When we are in class, teachers say, 'Listen, this is going to be on the exam.' Basically, the teacher is saying that nothing else really matters except those few questions on the test. Just a little internet surfing tells effects of 'teaching the test.' It does nothing to improve student potential. Students may answer specific questions on an exam, but they're unable to use that knowledge in a broader sense. Good teachers show you how to think everywhere. When students are able to think inside the classroom and out, that's true learning."

A reporter yelled out, "Why not take the test?"

"We do not have anything against tests in general. We protest how they use the tests. What is holding someone back going to do? A lot of kids who are held back drop out of school. Schools get in competitions to see who gets the best scores. School competition should not be the basis for our learning!"

"Are you prepared for the consequences of not taking the test?"

"We will go on to the 11th grade. We've proved ourselves in the classroom. The state better come up with something, because the entire 10th grade is here."

"Were your parents aware of today's events?"

"No, they were not, but as you can see, many parents are down here looking for their children. They might be able to make them go inside the school, but *we are not taking the test.*"

The students let out a big cheer.

"What's next?"

"Well, we are against all standardized tests as a way to segregate students. So, we're not taking the ACT, either. We'll meet school officials to discuss this.

"At this time, we have to go back into school. There has been enough said here. We will be taking more questions later. We want the school district and the university to be able to respond to our actions. Thank you very much."

The reporters kept yelling Loren's name as he walked calmly back into school, a small smile on his face.

Principal Who?

As Dr. Sarnacola got everyone inside the school, it became apparent the students were not going to test. Teachers, administrators and aids pleaded, but too much time had passed to be able to administer the state examination. The university president, Bill Mooney, under whose jurisdiction Johnson ultimately fell, called a meeting with me, Dr. Sarnacola, Mr. Simon, Coach D. and Mr. McClain in his office. He received a call from the state education superintendent.

As soon as we all sat down in his conference room, Mooney said furiously, "Who actually runs Johnson High? Should I be talking with Dr. Boyd, the principal or this Loren Wise boy?"

For a moment I wasn't sure if Mooney was being sarcastic. One of his insults finally hit me in the face. Mooney's sharp wit was only equaled by his ego. I sensed he was challenging us to a caustic debate. For most of the week, I resisted this, but now I didn't refuse. Mr. McClain, Coach D., Mr. Simon, and I listened to him speak about the recent events with hostility.

"How did this escalate?" Mooney asked repeatedly through the meeting.

I asked the same question to myself, at a loss. If I'd actually spent more time at the school, maybe I would have an answer.

After the events, I realized that I was more often in meetings with politicians, boosters, urban planners, union representatives and others than with my school's principal or in the classroom. Until that week, I'd never set foot in the principal's office. In fact, I was never involved at Johnson for any significant period that academic year.

Better to be in a school than a boardroom discussing a school. Our voices bounced off lifeless walls, with Mooney's leading.

A long, oval conference table stretched the length of the room. The cherry wood reflected a warped, ghostly image of Mooney. He sat opposite my seat. Although the table separated him from the rest of us, Mooney's shadow occasionally fell across the Johnson staff.

The president continued, "We have an overzealous, 15-year-old civil rights leader who wants more media attention than a politician. Johnson High has been featured on major newspapers, magazines, and television programs in the region. We also have some nationwide coverage. I'm reading stories about students who are running more covert operations than the CIA. You might as well say the Democratic National Convention was being held at an after-school assembly with no one noticing.

"My office has received dozens of emails, letters, texts and calls from irate parents who want to know if their child will graduate. I'm not going to count the media requests for interviews and information. The top colleges in the country are playing 'Good Samaritans' by offering scholarships to members of this class of graduate-ineligible freedom fighters. The state superintendent is worried that other districts or schools may follow suit."

The president paused and grabbed his forehead as if he had a weeklong migraine.

At that moment, I found the courage to interrupt.

"May I say something?"

Superintendent Mooney waved his hand, and I said, "Before this meeting goes further, I must say that the staff and faculty are working extremely hard to help bring positive closure to this drama. If anyone is to be held accountable, it's me."

Mooney said, "I agree. That's why I need you to take some personal responsibility for the situation."

"What's that supposed to mean?"

"We are getting heat from the media, parents and government. Something has to give."

I struggled to contain my anger.

However, Dr. Sarnacola said, "I have some of the hardest working teachers in the district, and—"

But Mooney said, "Can someone accept responsibility ever? A boy started this. Why can't you turn this around? I'll ask again. Who is running this school?"

People shifted in their seats, and Mooney looked at Dr. Sarnacola.

"Let me be frank with all of you. The first thing I tried to find out was how I could fire you and your entire staff. After careful deliberation, I came to the conclusion that the university may have to bail on the project."

I politely asked my staff to wait outside in the main office while I finished with President Mooney.

Mr. McClain whispered to me, "We don't deserve this. Let's go back and take care of our kids."

Coach D., who sat beside McClain, looked as if he were going to leap across the table and throttle Mooney. Mr. Simon stared defiantly into Mooney's eyes.

McClain turned slowly and gave an icy smile to Mooney. He tapped Simon on the chest to signal their departure. McClain,

Coach, and Simon headed to the door.

McClain turned back to me and said, "The kids don't deserve this."

After their exit, I calmed down and continued, "I must admit, Dr. Mooney, that I share many of the concerns expressed in this meeting, if you want to call this rant a meeting. However, I do not share your resentment, skepticism, or pessimism because we got kids to think about bigger questions and to fight for them."

"Exactly what questions would those be, Dr. Boyd?"

"Have you ever asked yourself during your educational career, what a good education is? I ask the question almost every day of my life, Dr. Mooney."

Mooney waited impatiently for my response.

"When you have kids, teachers, administrators and staff whose credibility and worth are constantly questioned, you ask hard questions. Dr. Mooney, what kind of education is going to get these children out of their reality and into a better one? I can see Loren's point."

Mooney interrupted, "I already know you're in cahoots with the boy. Your insubordination is apparent."

"As I was saying, I have to agree. What exactly are we teaching the children of Johnson High? The kids in my school need to learn that they matter in the world— something a 'state master plan' can't teach. Contrary to public perception, Johnson always graduated students who could toe the line with the best of them."

President Mooney said, "I ask myself questions as well. Why have Johnson students consistently scored poorly? Why do their parents go to sporting events instead of PTA meetings? Why do I hear excuses for failure?"

I said, "I hate to break the news to you, but the students, teachers, and staff of Johnson have a legacy of struggle. However, we're seeing the consequences of not rewarding that struggle."

"Am I going to hear some pitiful story about racism and the plight of your people? It's time to accept and *encourage* personal responsibility."

"Look in our books, Dr. Mooney! You would think black folks don't exist, except as freed slaves in Lincoln's time and in the civil rights era. Look at the tests they are required to master. Hear what universities are saying about our kids. Look at what employers say. Listen to what the middle-class whites and blacks say about our kids before they go to Catholic schools. These children are ignored. The effects of being ignored are evident."

"Intelligence isn't ignored Dr. Boyd."

"Not with these kids. Do you think Loren dropped out of the sky? Loren is one of many bright kids who can do anything you ask. The difference between Loren and the rest of the kids is that somewhere along the way Loren received and believed in a real education. Loren is liberated and he's exercising his freedom."

"I'll tell you what Loren is exercising. He is teaching other children that no matter what they do, students will not have the ability to do as well as whites on the test. I hear the same defeatist attitude in Loren that I hear in you. Because they're poor and black or brown or whatever, they cannot compete."

"You don't understand Loren. Loren is all about work, success, and progress. He is trying to get students to participate in and understand their world instead of blindly following what they're told. The reality is that if these students do what they're told or expected to do, they'll work in menial jobs, live for sports, join a gang, or live five minutes from where their parents live. Loren believes in his friends more than you and I ever will. He believes in the power of schools more than most. Most importantly he understands that in order for students like those at Johnson to succeed in *life*, they must understand the power of schools from a social, political and personal level."

"And that's not in our curriculum, Dr. Boyd. They're our schools. We control what's taught in them."

"No, we don't. They learn civics. They do not learn how to use that knowledge to change curriculum, to change policy, to help create a better citizenry. That is the education of liberation. Loren is teaching something that you can't afford to ignore: freedom."

Mooney decided to change focus. "Now that we wasted more of my time, let me remind you of your job. While you are walking around your school like Aristotle or Plato, try to remember that you have a job. You are supposed to *manage* a school using guidelines the district provides. Remember the *things* educational leaders and principals are supposed to do? If you have any credibility, you will lead this school on a path prescribed by the district, and you will persuade these kids to take the tests."

"Is that what you brought us here for— to cajole our students into taking tests?"

"Why else would you be here? I talked with the higher-ups in the state, and we can receive a waiver and take the test at a later date. Let's get these kids to do the right thing. When you do persuade the kids to take the tests, I want you to issue a statement condemning their actions as well-intentioned but misguided. I am asking you to do more leading and less philosophizing."

"In my twenty years of *leadership*, I definitely know the difference between management and education. Obviously, you don't recognize either concept."

"Why is it you have to play the role of teacher? Ever since we've met, you've played the role of some poor righteous teacher who eschews the institution while working in one. You envy

Loren because he is everything you want to be. However, your ideals flew out the window, and you eventually became part of the institution you criticize. You are a manager, Dr. Boyd. Don't forget it! Since we've adopted charter schools, I have been overly generous to Johnson. I believe their improvement is a reflection of my generosity. Attendance is up. Fights and violence are down. Teachers are more stable, and students' examination marks grow exponentially each year. If you do not lead as the district prescribes, I will not be so generous, and maybe Johnson won't be so successful. And neither will you."

"You don't have to worry Dr. Mooney," I said, quietly seething at his threat to not only ruin me, but more importantly, my children.

The Right to Parent and Feed

My lawyer Dorian Garnett was on the phone, and I braced myself. Constant calls from parents, administration and state officials kept me on edge. My anxieties heightened with each call since litigants had named me in four suits in as many months. None of the plaintiffs followed through, but the city's new arrangement created a particular climate of litigiousness. Because of our decentralized, fractured environment, someone with a complaint typically could not seek recourse beyond the school site. Teachers whose contracts were not renewed, parents who thought their child did not receive appropriate accommodations and professional activists trying to make larger statements all filed lawsuits for redress. The court became the mediator.

I said, "Just tell me."

Dorian replied, "Ms. Cassandra Constance, mother of Brandy Stokes, filed a lawsuit yesterday against you and the school."

"For what?"

"Ms. Constance's lawyer is arguing that banning her lunches violated the family's constitutional rights to parent. The mother felt she should have been allowed to give Brandy the food she wanted because that's how Ms. Constance wanted to rear her."

"That's ridiculous. The mother is killing her. That greasy chicken has ballooned a 9-year-old to 180 pounds and she'll likely develop type-II diabetes. The girl's not even 5 feet tall!"

"They're saying her health isn't an issue since she wasn't diagnosed by a doctor."

Finishing Dorian's sentence, I said, "The school clinic's nurse said her weight IS a health issue. The girl is practically handicapped. She can't climb stairs to class without being winded and sweating."

"I don't *think* this can go anywhere..."

"I'm so sick of this shit. We're talking morbid obesity in a 9-year-old, and *I'm* being sued. I should sue Ms. Constance."

"Look, I'll call when I hear more, but this is what you signed up for."

"Now there, you're wrong."

Brief Meeting

I asked Dr. Sarnacola to round up Mr. Simon and Loren in his office. Dr. Sarnacola was still fuming from Mooney's meeting a few days earlier. I couldn't get Mooney or Loren out of my mind. I had to talk to the boy about the tests.

After a short staff meeting, we invited Loren in.

I said, "Hello Loren. How are you holding up?"

Loren sounded sullen. "All right."

"Have a seat."

Loren moved toward the worn chair in front of Dr. Sarnacola's desk.

"How is your family? What does Ms. Rena have to say about all this?"

Loren said, "Mom is OK."

I sat and looked at Loren, searching his face for some revelation. There was none. I didn't want to push him in the wrong direction.

It was clear he'd expected to be called in, so I said, "I called you in to check on you and to give you some advice."

"I know what you're about to say, Dr. Boyd. You want me and the rest to take the test."

"Loren, I think we've developed a pretty good relationship.

I trust you. Dr. Sarnacola and Mr. Simon trust you. I think you trust me." I paused for validation.

"Yes," he said, warily.

"Good. First I want you to know I spoke with the president of the university and with the state superintendent, who informed us that the state is willing to make an exemption for Johnson school. The state is going to set another date for you and your classmates."

Loren sat silently digesting my offer.

"Before you speak, I just want you to know how I feel about the situation."

I paused, moved closer in my chair and said, "I am so proud of you. You've done what people in this city should have done since forever. You're taking your destiny in your own hands."

Loren looked up.

I said, "Continue to live with purpose. I will never forget that press conference. I felt so proud for you at the championship. And for Clarence, too. He was magnificent. Clarence had a focus few people can garner. My heart pumped a thousand beats per second those last hundred meters. You've done everything we've asked. Do you understand, Loren?"

"Yes sir."

I eased back in my seat and looked Loren in the eyes and said, "However, you have to learn how to pick your battles. This is a fight you can't win. I need you to take the tests and do well."

I could see Loren's disappointment.

I continued, "You've made your point. This school and city are better for what you've done. Now *you* have to reap the benefits. Just think when colleges see your grades, test scores and your feats. Forget an essay. Show them the news clippings and interviews."

I laughed.

"But you have to take the test to get into college and continue what you've already started. Don't be a martyr."

I got out of my seat and moved toward Loren. He rose from his seat. Loren let out a deep sigh of relief.

Where Did the Teachers Go?

The Post Katrina Education Reform Conference hosted by the college of education and the university's Lindy Boggs Conference Center brought dozens of researchers from across the country to present empirical and theoretical papers on a variety of reform topics. My excitement encouraged me to go over to the site hours earlier to see if my colleague David Dixson needed assistance in the final hours before the opening dinner. The country needed this conference as the reform movement outpaced, out-resourced and out-promoted research organizations during the same time period.

As conference planners prepared for their guests, a small child no older than five played exuberantly with a fifty-something black secretary. I watched intently as her movements reminded me of the woman who raised me. The secretary's smile and loving hand gestures made me pause. When I saw how engaged and comforted the small child was with the secretary, I imagined providing that comfort for every student.

When the child's parent scooped her child away, I walked up to the woman and introduced myself. "Hello, I'm Isaac Boyd. I work with David, who is organizing the conference."

"Oh Dr. Boyd, it's a pleasure to meet you. I'm Mattie Woods.

I've heard so much about your work in the schools and think you're doing an excellent job. I'm proud of you."

"Thank you, but you should consider becoming a teacher. I watched you from across the hall, and you worked so well with that child. You just have that gift that we look for in education."

Ms. Woods said, "I was a kindergarten and first-grade teacher for the old Orleans Parish. I worked at Armand Lanusse for twenty years. I was let go after the storm."

Feelings can't be measured in seconds, but in between her sentences, a deep sadness sank in my gut like a meal I was forced to eat. Ms. Woods was our mother, our caretaker, our teacher. Ms Woods was the collateral damage of fast-paced innovation.

My despondence must have been obvious. But her eyes woke me from my stupor as if to snap her fingers in front of my face. Like my mom, she said, "It's okay. I've moved on."

I asked for her story.

"I was bouncing back and forth between Little Rock and here. My home was wiped out, so I couldn't get a jump on the hiring process. By the time I got back, positions were filled."

I said, "Please, send me your résumé. I know I have a place for you."

"I'm happy for now working in the conference center. Don't worry."

"I can feel how good you are."

She laughed and said, "Thank you baby, but it's your turn. I'm tired of the battles."

"That's my job to fight. Teachers shouldn't be in those political skirmishes. We need people like you in the classroom."

"You know it doesn't work like that." A brief silence confirmed her assertion. "Let me ask you this. Are the schools really getting better?"

I looked at her point blank and said, "They are."

"Then I'm okay. I have to be. If someone can do a better job than me, then I need to step aside for the sake of children. It just hurts when you believe people are given chances to work just because they weren't part of the old system."

"I know. We have to develop a grow-your-own teachers program in the city."

"You're on to something, Dr. Boyd, but it's not just about locals versus outsiders. You weren't born here. Like it or not. You eventually became one of us."

I still couldn't vision myself in a Saints jersey.

She continued, "Sometimes the reformers sound so ignorant. We host many of their meetings, and they don't even think I could be a former teacher. I don't tell anybody, though. People think we just disappeared." Realizing that I made the same error, I stayed silent. She continued, "They're so blind. I would rather be uneducated than miseducated."

Anxious to catch her drift I asked, "How?"

"When you're uneducated, at least your mind is open. When you're miseducated, you will kill yourself and others trying to prove the wrong answer.

"This city has been miseducated into thinking that black people can't do for ourselves. Black people believe it. White people believe it. No matter what fancy innovation we bring to Orleans, we bark up the same magnolia."

I asked, "How can we make it right?"

"I just want people to believe in me. I didn't go to Harvard, but I can contribute. I just want to be considered."

If our reforms could not distinguish between Ms. Woods and someone with no teaching skills, then what good was it? I hoped reform and community would be partners. Would we eventually trust the graduates of reform to teaching and leadership positions? I left with the agony Ms. Woods tried to relieve me from. I considered I might be furthering the miseducation of a city.

Not this School

On an unusually cool, dry Sunday morning, my lawyer, Dorian, and I sat outdoors at a popular coffee shop in Mid-City discussing the chicken lady lawsuit that would probably be dismissed. Relaxed in my workout clothes, this meeting was to be the only excitement I'd planned that day. However, as the first fire truck in a series screamed by the outdoor patio, I smelled something burning. Before the alarm, I dismissed the scent as something from the coffee shop. However, the sounds of sirens blasting around us told me otherwise.

I looked at my cell phone to see if I'd received any calls; I hadn't. I asked my lawyer the same. He said no. I called my principals individually. None of them received a call from our alarm provider to alert them of a fire at their schools. Feeling a moment of relief, I excused myself from the meeting to do a drive-by.

While driving, my cell phone buzzed against my hip. When I saw Mr. Simon's name on the screen, my fear rose. "What's going on?"

Mr. Simon replied, exasperated, "Dr. Boyd, you have to get down to Treme."

"Why?"

"There's a fire at Armand Lanusse."

"Who says?"

"I was hanging with some of the teachers from Prep at the Streetcar Festival, and they got the word from Brian Rice. They've blocked off some of the streets, so we're walking up Esplanade right now."

"Okay, thanks for the call. Be safe."

I was already headed to the school. After a few minutes on Esplanade, I saw flashing lights, the barricades and dark smoke clouds looming over Treme. I pulled the truck over and began the short walk to Armand Lanusse School. As I neared it, the smell of burning wood and plastic was thick enough to start me coughing. I could see neighbors making their way to the source of the smell. Bike riders whizzed past to see the action. I began to jog to the site.

For the last few blocks I started walking. The crowd made it impossible to move quickly, and I wanted to prepare myself. Children sprinted across streets, not heeding calls from elders to stay on porches. Neighbors convened toward the fire as if they were headed to a second-line funeral procession. Fearing the worst, I hoped the building wouldn't have significant damage. But, as I turned the block, I saw nothing but flames shooting from the roof and water uselessly trying to beat them back. I weaved between onlookers to get a spot by the barrier.

On the periphery of the school, hundreds of neighbors watched. Orange flames reflected off their sable skins. The spectacle of the fire distracted me from cries in the background. Everyone stood as if watching a bonfire. It became obvious which students in the crowd attended the school. They were in tears, some clutching their parents. I saw Baba Karim standing across the street, staring intently. Mr. Simon stood a few feet from Karim. As I gazed over the audience, I noticed Rice beside me. We nodded. Rice shook his head in disbelief and disgust. We both stared, thinking about our futures and the school's future.

After about fifteen minutes, Rice turned to me and said, "They don't want change. They don't want change."

He walked through the crowd toward his home in Treme.

The Storm Season Returns Every Year

While listening to a student choir in a large multipurpose room during the Urban League Schools Expo, Dr. Sarnacola sent a text message: "PLEASE CALL!" I exited the room to search for a private area to talk.

The Schools Expo drew hundreds of parents who sought to enroll their children in a new school. School choice had started to bear fruit. Because attendance zone restrictions were lifted after the storm, families can apply for enrollment in any public school in the city. If more families apply than seats are available, then the school must conduct a lottery. Parents equipped themselves with information so they could decide where to place their children. The event reminded me of open-air markets and swap meets.

School leaders needed to fill their rosters to be financially solvent. Instead of dollar-store merchandise, teachers and principals sold their schools. Bazaar-style showrooms put schools' strong points on display.

The event provided an opportunity for a fractured school system to build a new type of community. A network of mothers traded rumors, experiences and stories about various schools. Thousands bumped into each other throughout the complex. It was the kind of chaos I enjoyed. Parents and children filled hallways. I smiled as I weaved between parents juggling school applications, giveaways and information. Outside was just as crowded. Performing bands and cheerleaders filled whatever space was left with sound.

I walked to the far end of the parking lot and found enough quiet to return my call. Sarnacola told me that freshman Chuck Hanson took a picture with his cell phone of two teachers making out in the library and that students were distributing it among themselves.

I asked Sarnacola, "Are parents aware?"

He replied, "That's how I found out. Parents are calling, and they are upset."

"I can feel another lawsuit coming. Couldn't those teachers wait to get home? I'm getting tired of this lack of discipline. I'm almost willing to say fire them … But let's talk about this later. In fact, refer this to the lawyer. I got better things to do than talk about inappropriate teachers. I was having a good day. I don't need this."

Sarnacola said, "This is a little more complicated."

"What's more complicated than referring it to the lawyer?"

"I am going to call you in a few hours so we can talk."

"Look, I've been sued by parents who can't stop feeding their kid fried chicken. I don't want to deal with more parent complaints. If counsel says termination, then do it. I really want to get back to the event."

Sarnacola quickly said, "There is one major problem." I shook my head knowing that nothing comes easy.

He continued, "The pictures are of Mr. Simon and a teacher from Prep."

It took me a few seconds to grasp what was said.

"Mr. Simon had his pants down."

I could not believe this. How could he make such a mistake? I knew better than to rush to judgment, but I felt Simon had betrayed my trust. In addition, the ramifications of one of the top charter schools in the city with a teacher having sex in the school would be a serious political blow.

Autonomy can help bury many student and teacher issues, but the idea of a leader and its board burying sexual pictures was impossible. At least it was two adults and not a student and teacher, was the best I could comfort myself with.

Sarnacola repeated, "What should I do?"

I know I sounded depressed when I said, "Inform counsel and let him handle it."

Sarnacola said, "You know he'll recommend firing him."

"I know. I know." I paused and then quietly let out an angry, "Fuck!"

Sarnacola replied, "I'm sorry, Isaac."

There was nothing more to say.

If only I worked in a church or a private school, these issues could be dealt with internally. Public schools are stages for community missteps. I did not want a pelting from the media. I knew that choosing not to act was more than a logistical or legal matter. I knew that pulling Mr. Simon's coattails could potentially disrupt an investigation. However, I was tired. I didn't have the energy to fix the situation. Most of the craziness public schools had before the storm found new homes afterward.

Numb from the news, the crowds of parents faded before me. I could not think. I kept asking, when will the storms stop? I imagined the bloodletting the daily rag would start. I could hear spiteful chatter from people who never liked Simon anyway. I could hear Simon's weak explanation. At that moment, I realized that I just wanted to be an aloof professor.

As I walked toward the performance areas, a woman as ugly as my current situation yelled at one of her family members about losing a voucher for school supplies. She had a scarred face that drugs and pressures of the ghetto probably shaped. Expletives and grammatical errors flowed from her dry lips.

She used the wheel chair ramp to loudly castigate a young boy of about 10.

"I told you to fucking get another bag! We ain't come out here to get nothing! Tell them you lost the voucher."

I saw eyes roll from adults in the vicinity. I took a deep breath and motioned toward the woman. The woman was beyond shame. A grandmother next to me said, "There's always got to be one."

She smiled as if to say good luck.

I walked briskly toward the pair. As I moved closer, she reached into her backpack. She pulled out a leather belt covered with duct-tape. She looked defiant.

"I don't care. I'll whoop your ass right here. Bring me out here for nothing."

As she placed the buckle in her palm and made a loop with the belt around her hand, I grabbed and held the belt to prevent her from swinging.

"Ma'am, ma'am. This is not the place. Please put the belt in the bag, or you'll have to leave."

"You don't own this place. You don't tell me what to do."

Using a forceful but controlled tone, I said, "My name is Dr. Isaac Boyd, I am the Associate Dean of the College of Education here at UNO. I am hosting this event. Please place the belt in the bag."

Though she heard me, she asked, "Who are you?"

Another adult, possibly her daughter, tried to calm her down.

The woman was scared now.

I continued, "Ma'am, we cannot have cursing or violence here. There are children around."

The daughter said softly, touching her other arm lightly, "He's right, Ma."

I slowly let go of the belt, and she stuffed it deep in her bag.

I then politely asked, "Now, what happened?"

"My boy left his new school bag and voucher by the space walk, and somebody took it. Now he don't have neither and they sayin' he can't get another voucher or bag," she practically snarled through the few teeth left in her mouth. She might've been 35 but looked a beat up 60. The older daughter was about 19.

I started looking for an Urban League staffer to see if I could get the family another bag and school-supply voucher. I implored Briana to help them. She knew the family and would see if another could be given. However, the League provided a limited number on a first-come, first-served basis and many families awaiting vouchers and supplies still stood in line. As a board member, I knew my request would be granted, but I also realized that I took away another family's opportunity for school supplies.

I shook my head and said to myself, "New Orleans is not ready to change." When I said that, I knew it was time to return to teaching college. I tried to find the politically correct reasons to give my bosses so that I would not burn bridges or future opportunities. None of what I concocted felt authentic, but it would probably serve its purpose. How could I say I was tired of running the treadmill; tired of fighting the same battles in different places; tired of fighting the same people for different reasons. However, today I did something that I'd previously claimed would be the reason for resignation— thought that the city didn't want to change. I made my decision to quit because I decided to stop fighting.

Sometimes you know when it's time. You feel it in your bones. I never had troubles moving on in the past, but a lack of reasonable voices kept me in the mix longer than I'd planned. I could not continue to live in the constant cycle of 60-minute meetings. I needed to reflect.

Where was education headed? Where was I headed? What was the end game? I was so desperate to change New Orleans schools that I allowed myself to become something I wasn't. I had become a middleman, stuck between reformers' latent mistrust of local people and preservationists unyielding denial of their contributions to a failed school system. So desperate, I began to fight a battle I couldn't win. Reason and reconciliation are not appropriate weapons in the educational Crusades.

My blackness and my desire for radical change painted bull's eyes on me, front and back. Now, however, I would gladly fall on my own sword. I became a black pawn who could be easily deposed by a Rex or Zulu. Along the way, I became a formidable player, but now I was simply repackaging what they had been doing to each other for years. I never felt like an outsider, until the day I decided to give up. I felt like going to Pittsburgh, but I also realized New Orleans was my new home.

I started walking. I felt defeated among people who needed a champion. I could no longer fight. I thought, there had to be another way to change.

As I moved through the group formed around the drama, a young man about 21 called my name. I could hear strength in his voice.

This dark brown, square-jawed son looked me dead in the eyes, demanding respect.

He extended his hand and asked, "Dr. Boyd, may I speak with you privately?"

I replied, "Certainly. Let's go in the parking lot."

I returned to the area where Sarnacola informed me about Mr. Simon. I assumed that he was the older brother of a student who may have been suspended. I tried to make small talk as we moved through the crowd.

When we finally reached our destination, I asked, "How may I help you?"

"Dr. Boyd, my name is William Toussaint. My sister Tania Robinson, who is in Johnson High School, said you could help me."

A young girl who looked familiar stood about 20 feet in the background. I glanced, to get a closer look, but I wanted to give Toussaint my full attention.

I replied, "Yes."

Toussaint seemed uncomfortable.

He said, "I wanted to see if you can allow someone in your school."

He spoke very carefully so as to not make a grammatical error. His New Orleans malapropisms seemed to strain under the effort. However, I could sense something at work inside him. He looked at the girl in the distance.

"That's easy." I looked at the slender, brown girl who seemed to wear stress over her tight jeans. She pulled down her T-shirt as it rose above her waistline.

I looked toward the girl and asked Toussaint, "Is that Dr. Prevost? Is that Jarnee Prevost? Is she your girlfriend?"

Surprised and thrown, he corrected my assumption. "Jarnee is not my girlfriend. I met her while stationed in Arkansas."

It became clear the reverence and uneasiness I felt were signs that he had just begun to grow into his military role. Toussaint did not stand like other males his age from New Orleans.

I asked, "What branch are you serving in?"

"Army, sir."

"How is that working for you?"

"Good. I'm going to college afterwards." His response reflected a typical path inner-city males took to get their lives on track.

I continued to talk while Jarnee hung in the background. I looked in her direction and said, "Does she need to get into Johnson?"

"Yes."

"You just got back to New Orleans?"

"Yes."

"How do you know her? Where are her parents?"

"She had a falling out with her parents. Her family has a lot of problems." Toussaint said definitively, "Jarnee is a good girl. She needs a good school."

"Where did you meet her?" As soon as I asked the question, I thought— did I really want to know?

He replied, "I met her in Little Rock."

"Where's she staying?"

"She's going to live with my mom in New Orleans."

"Your mom is OK with that?"

"Yes."

I didn't remember Jarnee's age, but New Orleans emancipates students at 16. However, the idea that a military man transported a possible minor across state lines bothered me. I looked deep into his eyes.

I then turned towards Jarnee and said, "Jarnee, let me talk to you privately for a second."

I turned to Toussaint and said, "Excuse me."

I cautiously gave Jarnee a hug knowing I left her with her child. "Hello, Jarnee. How have you been? How's Talana?"

Jarnee looked down at my feet. Slightly above a whisper, she replied, "Talana, my baby, is with a woman in Little Rock. I'm going to get her after I'm settled in New Orleans."

I regained eye contact and said, "Where have you been? How do you know that Toussaint guy?"

"He met me at the mall. We're just friends."

"Why would he drive you hundreds of miles to enroll you in school?"

She knew she needed to say something that would keep me from contacting authorities.

Jarnee responded, "He wants me to be safe."

"Is your mother abusive?"

"Yes, sir."

"Jarnee, I can get you into school, but you do know that I am going to have my social worker check your story."

"Yes, sir." Jarnee looked up to me with as much confidence as an abused teen could muster and said, "OK."

"What do you think of Toussaint?"

"He's very nice."

I still wanted to know the nature of their relationship.

I asked, "Now where did you meet him?"

"We met at the Dairy Queen in a mall in Little Rock."

"How did he learn about your situation?"

"We talked for hours. When I told him that me and my sister went there every day, he asked, 'Why?'"

"I said we were trying to stay away from home."

"Where is your sister?"

"She didn't want to leave."

"What's going to happen to her?"

"Same thing that always happens— gets slapped around."

I looked towards Toussaint and called him over. I then asked, "If she and her baby stay with your parents, where are you going?"

"I am being deployed to Iraq in two weeks. She'll help fill an empty house. They won't mind."

I tried not to look worried but was sure this was evident. I extended my hand and said, "Godspeed."

I almost forgot why we were there.

I let the two know that I would make immediate arrangements to get Jarnee into school.

After a sober discussion about going to war, Toussaint asked me, "Will you help me when I get back? I want to go to UNO."

I replied, "I'll be here waiting for all of you."

Also Available from UNO Press:

William Christenberry: Art & Family by J. Richard Gruber (2000)
The El Cholo Feeling Passes by Fredrick Barton (2003)
A House Divided by Fredrick Barton (2003)
Coming Out the Door for the Ninth Ward edited by Rachel Breunlin from The Neighborhood Story Project series (2006)
The Change Cycle Handbook by Will Lannes (2008)
Cornerstones: Celebrating the Everyday Monuments & Gathering Places of New Orleans edited by Rachel Breunlin, from The Neighborhood Story Project series (2008)
A Gallery of Ghosts by John Gery (2008)
Hearing Your Story: Songs of History and Life for Sand Roses by Nabile Farès translated by Peter Thompson, from The Engaged Writers Series (2008)
The Imagist Poem: Modern Poetry in Miniature edited by William Pratt from The Ezra Pound Center for Literature series (2008)
The Katrina Papers: A Journal of Trauma and Recovery by Jerry W. Ward, Jr. from The Engaged Writers Series (2008)
On Higher Ground: The University of New Orleans at Fifty by Dr. Robert Dupont (2008)
Us Four Plus Four: Eight Russian Poets Conversing translated by Don Mager (2008)
Voices Rising: Stories from the Katrina Narrative Project edited by Rebeca Antoine (2008)
Gravestones (Lápidas) by Antonio Gamoneda, translated by Donald Wellman from The Engaged Writers Series (2009)
The House of Dance and Feathers: A Museum by Ronald W. Lewis by Rachel Breunlin & Ronald W. Lewis, from The Neighborhood Story Project series (2009)
I hope it's not over, and good-by: Selected Poems of Everette Maddox by Everette Maddox (2009)
Portraits: Photographs in New Orleans 1998-2009 by Jonathan Traviesa (2009)
Theoretical Killings: Essays & Accidents by Steven Church (2009)
Voices Rising II: More Stories from the Katrina Narrative Project edited by Rebeca Antoine (2010)
Rowing to Sweden: Essays on Faith, Love, Politics, and Movies by Fredrick Barton (2010)
Dogs in My Life: The New Orleans Photographs of John Tibule Mendes (2010)
Understanding the Music Business: A Comprehensive View edited by Harmon Greenblatt & Irwin Steinberg (2010)
The Fox's Window by Naoko Awa, translated by Toshiya Kamei (2010)
A Passenger from the West by Nabile Farès, translated by Peter Thompson from The Engaged Writers Series (2010)
The Schüssel Era in Austria: Contemporary Austrian Studies, Volume 18 edited by Günter Bischof & Fritz Plasser (2010)
The Gravedigger by Rob Magnuson Smith (2010)
Everybody Knows What Time It Is by Reginald Martin (2010)
When the Water Came: Evacuees of Hurricane Katrina by Cynthia Hogue & Rebecca Ross from The Engaged Writers Series (2010)
Aunt Alice Vs. Bob Marley by Kareem Kennedy, from The Neighborhood Story Project series (2010)
Houses of Beauty: From Englishtown to the Seventh Ward by Susan Henry from The Neighborhood Story Project series (2010)
Signed, The President by Kenneth Phillips, from The Neighborhood Story Project series (2010)
Beyond the Bricks by Daron Crawford & Pernell Russell from The Neighborhood Story Project series (2010)
Green Fields: Crime, Punishment, & a Boyhood Between by Bob Cowser, Jr., from the Engaged Writers Series (2010)

New Orleans: The Underground Guide by Michael Patrick Welch & Alison Fensterstock (2010)
Writer in Residence: Memoir of a Literary Translater by Mark Spitzer (2010)
Open Correspondence: An Epistolary Dialogue by Abdelkébir Khatibi and Rita El Khayat, translated by Safoi Babana-Hampton, Valérie K. Orlando, Mary Vogl from The Engaged Writers Series (2010)
Black Santa by Jamie Bernstein (2010)
From Empire to Republic: Post-World-War-I Austria: Contemporary Austrian Studies, Volume 19 edited by Günter Bischof, Fritz Plasser and Peter Berger (2010)
Vegetal Sex (O Sexo Vegetal) by Sergio Medeiros, translated by Raymond L.Bianchi (2010)
Dream-crowned (Traumgekrönt) by Rainer Maria Rilke, translated by Lorne Mook (2010)
Wounded Days (Los Días Heridos) by Leticia Luna, translated by Toshiya Kamei (2010) from The Engaged Writers Series (2010)
Beyond the Islands by Alicia Yánez Cossio, translated by Amalia Gladhart
Enridged by Brian Richards, Contemporary Poetry
The Garden Path: The Miseducation of a City by Andre M. Perry
Together by Julius Chingono and John Eppel. The Engaged Writers Series
The Combination by Ashley Nelson, Contemporary Poety

unopress.org